SEP 2020

S0-ACT-675

WITHDRAWN

IN AN ABSENT
DREAM

Center Point
Large Print

Also by Seanan McGuire and available from Center Point Large Print:

Every Heart a Doorway
Down Among the Sticks and Bones
Beneath the Sugar Sky

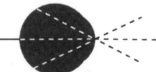

**This Large Print Book carries the
Seal of Approval of N.A.V.H.**

IN AN ABSENT
DREAM

SEANAN McGUIRE

Mount Laurel Library
100 Walt Whitman Avenue
Mount Laurel, NJ 08054-9539
856-234-7319
www.mountlaurellibrary.org

Center Point Large Print
Thorndike, Maine

This Center Point Large Print edition
is published in the year 2020 by arrangement with
Tor-Forge Books.

Copyright © 2018 by Seanan McGuire.

All rights reserved.

This is a work of fiction. All of the characters,
organizations, and events portrayed
in this novel are either products of the author's
imagination or are used fictitiously.

The text of this Large Print edition is unabridged.
In other aspects, this book may vary
from the original edition.
Printed in the United States of America
on permanent paper.
Set in 16-point Times New Roman type.

ISBN: 978-1-64358-560-4

The Library of Congress has cataloged this record
under Library of Congress Control Number: 2019957010

For Talis,
who knows the way
to the Goblin Market

Come buy, come buy:
Our grapes fresh from the vine,
Pomegranates full and fine,
Dates and sharp bullaces,
Rare pears and greengages,
Damsons and bilberries,
Taste them and try:
Currants and gooseberries,
Bright-fire-like barberries,
Figs to fill your mouth,
Citrons from the South,
Sweet to tongue and sound to eye;
Come buy, come buy.
—CHRISTINA ROSSETTI,
GOBLIN MARKET

IN AN ABSENT
DREAM

PART I
WHAT WE WOULD REAP

1 A VERY ORDINARY GARDEN

1964

In a house, on a street, in a town ordinary enough in every aspect to cross over its own roots and become remarkable, there lived a girl named Katherine Victoria Lundy. She had a brother, six years older and a little bit wild in the way of boys who could look over their shoulders and see the shadow of a war standing there, its jaws open and hungry. She had a sister, six years younger and a little bit shy in the way of children who had yet to decide whether they would be timid or brave, kind or cruel. She had two parents who loved her and a small ginger cat who purred when she stroked its back, and everything was lovely, and everything was terrible.

Like the town where she lived, where she had been born, and where she was beginning to feel, in a slow and abstract way, that she would someday die, Katherine—never Kate, never Kitty, never anything but Katherine, sensible Katherine, up-and-down Katherine, as dependable as a sundial whittling away the summer afternoons—was ordinary enough to have become remarkable entirely without noticing it. Had she been pressed on the matter she might, after protesting that there was nothing remarkable about her, have suggested her own sixth birthday as the moment of the twist.

We must go back a little beyond the beginning, then, to learn; to observe. What are we here for, after all, if not for that? So:

Little Katherine, her mother's belly round and ripe as a Halloween pumpkin, bulging with the impending harvest of her sister, sitting prim at the picnic table her parents have set up in the backyard. There is a cake, slightly lopsided, frosted in lemon buttercream that smells sweet and sour in the same breath, impossibly tempting and glittering with sugar crystals. There are gifts, a small pile of them, wrapped in brightly colored paper recycled from other birthdays, other holidays. There is her brother, twelve years old and eyeing the cake with a pirate's hunger, ready to pillage its depths the second he is given leave. There are so many things here, paper streamers and smiling parents and the distant scent of bonfires burning in the fields. There are so many things that it would be easy to miss what should be obvious: to miss what isn't here.

There are no other children. There is Katherine, and there is her brother, who has somehow already gotten frosting on the tip of his nose, and that is where it stops. As if to add insult to injury, the sound of laughter drifts over the fence from a neighbor's yard, where half a dozen children from Katherine's school have gathered to play. If not for the tempting lure of cake, her brother would already be out the gate and gone, off to join what sounds like a far better party.

Her father, who is principal of the local elementary school, scowls at the fence but says nothing. He believes there is no malice in the timing of this event, that Katherine, overcome by the shyness that sometimes consumes children her age, failed to hand out invitations. He has even seen a few of them, ripped in half and stuffed into the kitchen garbage, where a cascade of eggshells and coffee grounds was not quite enough to hide them. He thinks this has nothing to do with him, with the way he enforces discipline and guides his students with a heavy, steady hand. After all, Katherine's older brother had birthday parties, and they were well attended by his peers.

(The fact that he became principal two years ago, and that his son has not requested a party since, only the company of a few beloved chums and an afternoon at the movies or the carnival, does not occur to him.)

Her mother, who is so pregnant that her world has narrowed and widened at the same time, becoming a funhouse tunnel through which she must pass before she can be rewarded with a baby's cry and the sweet simplicity of raising an infant, an innocent babe who will not yet share the trials and tribulations of the older children, has a better idea of what her husband's job has meant for her daughter's friendships. She remembers sweetly smiling children with sticky fingers, trailing along in a pack, Katherine never at the head or the rear, but somewhere in the comfortable, unremarkable middle. She remembers when they stopped coming around.

(She remembers, but she has a house to keep and a baby to bear, and somehow calling their mothers and finding back alleys into camaraderie has never been enough of a priority to nudge her into action. There are only so many hours in the day.)

The year is 1962. Katherine is six years old, two years after the doorbell stopped ringing in her name, two years away from the door we have come to see swing open. There is a choice here, hanging like smoke in the autumn air. She can cry for the friends she doesn't have, mourn for the games she isn't playing, or she can let them go. She can be the kind of girl who doesn't need anyone else to keep her happy, the kind of girl who smiles at adults and keeps her own company. She can be content.

"Blow out the candles, Katherine," urges her father, and she does, and she's happy. She's happy.

16

There: that wasn't so difficult, and it *mattered*. Small things often do. A single pebble in the road can go unnoticed until it becomes stuck inside a horse's hoof, and then oh, the damage it can do. This was a pebble; this was where things began the slow, stony process of changing.

Katherine walked away from her sixth birthday party with a smile on her face and the scent of lemon frosting clinging to her fingers, the ghost of sugar once enjoyed. She understood now, that the other children weren't coming; that they would always be shadowy voices on the other side of a fence, refusing to let her through, refusing to let her in. She understood that she had, for whatever reason, been rejected from their society, and would not be readmitted unless something fundamental in the world chose to shift in its foundations, widening itself, rebirthing her into someone they could care for.

But she didn't *want* to be someone they could care for. She didn't want to be a Kate or a Kitty or even a Kat—all perfectly lovely, serviceable names, for perfectly lovely, serviceable people. People she already knew, at six years of age, that she didn't want to be. She was Katherine Lundy. Her family loved her as Katherine Lundy. If the children in the yard next door or on the playground couldn't find her worth loving the same way, she wasn't going to change for them.

If this seems unusually mature for a child of

six, it is, and it is not. Children are capable of grasping complex ideas long before most people give them credit for, wrapping them in a soothing layer of nonsense and illogical logic. To be a child is to be a visitor from another world muddling your way through the strange rules of this one, where up is always up, even when it would make more sense for it to be down, or backward, or sideways. Yet children can see the functionality of grief or understand the complexities of a parent's love without hesitating. They find their way through. They *deduce*. Katherine had *deduced,* when the other children called her snobby or mean for not wanting them to cut her name short, when they had told her they couldn't play with her because her daddy was the boss of their teacher and she would be a snitch someday, wait and see, that they weren't going to change their minds about her.

Katherine was also, in many ways, a remarkable child. All children are: no two are sliced from the same clean cloth. It is simply that for some children, their remarkable attributes will take the form of being able to locate the nearest mud puddle without being directed toward it, even when there has been no rain for a month or more, or being able to scream in registers that cause the neighborhood bats to lose control of themselves and soar into kitchen windows. Katherine's remarkability took the form of a quiet self-assuredness, a conviction that as long as she followed the rules, she could find her way through any maze, pass cleanly through any storm.

She was not the type to seek adventure, no, but she was well-enough acquainted with the shapes it might take. Shortly after the birthday where she had blown out the candles and made her choices, she discovered the pure joy of reading for pleasure, and was rarely—if ever—seen without a book in her hand. Even in slumber, she was often to be found clutching a volume with one slender hand, her fingers wrapped tight around its spine, as if she feared to wake into a world where all books had been forgotten and removed, and this book might become the last she had to linger over.

In the way of bookish children, she carried her books into trees and along the banks of chuckling creeks, weaving her way along their slippery shores with the sort of grace that belongs only to bibliophiles protecting their treasures. Through the words on the page she followed Alice down rabbit holes and Dorothy into tornados, solved mysteries alongside Trixie Belden and Nancy Drew, flew with Peter to Neverland, and made a wonderful journey to a Mushroom Planet. Her family was reasonably well-off, and there was no shortage of books, either through the shops or the library, which seemed to be entirely without limits.

Two years trickled by, one page at a time. Had she been someone else's daughter, she might have found herself the butt of cruel jokes played by her peers, called "suck-up" or even the newly coined and hence still-cruel "nerd." But her father was the principal, and the other children understood very well that the place for casual cruelty was outside his field of vision: the worst she was ever called where anyone might hear was "teacher's pet," which she took, not as an insult, but rather as a statement of fact. She was Katherine, she was the teacher's pet, and when she grew up, she was going to be a librarian, because she couldn't imagine knowing there was a job that was all about *books* and not wanting to do it.

No one ever asked if she was happy. It was evident enough that she was, that she had made her choices and set her courses even before she understood what they were, and if her mother sometimes wished that Katherine had more friends—or that she were more interested in babies than books, since it would have been nice to have some help around the house—she never said so. She loved the daughter she had, books and soft strangeness and rigid adherence to the rules and all. Katherine wasn't lonely. That was all that mattered.

(Her father, it may be noted, wished nothing for his daughter, because he saw nothing strange about the way she was shaping herself, inside the soft walls of her upbringing. Her brother was playing peewee baseball and trading cards; her younger sister was talking and walking and doing all the other things one expects from a toddler trending into childhood. Katherine was quiet and biddable and studious and modest. Katherine didn't run around with the wrong sort, tear her dresses or scuff her shoes. That this was because Katherine wasn't running around with any sort at all seemed to escape him, tucked away with all the other things he didn't want to think about. There were a surprising number of those. Like all adults, he had his secrets.)

At eight years old, Katherine Lundy already knew the shape of her entire life. Could have drawn it on a map if pressed: the long highways of education, the soft valleys of settling down. She assumed, in her practical way, that a husband would appear one day, summoned out of the ether like a necessary milestone, and she would work at the library while he worked someplace equally sensible, and they would have children of their own, because that was how the world was structured. Children begat adults begat children, now and forever, amen. She was in no hurry to reach those terrifying heights of adulthood; she assumed they would happen somewhere around the eighth grade, which was impossibly far away, and happened on the junior high school campus, where her father held no sway.

She wasn't sure exactly what one was supposed to *do* with a husband, but she was quite sure her father wouldn't want to be there when she did it, as he sometimes made dire comments about girls who played with boys while they were all at the dinner table, always followed by a smile and a comment of "But *you* would never do that, would you, Katherine?"

She had assured him over and over that she wouldn't, even though logic stated that one day she would, since boys became husbands and normal women had husbands and he wanted her to be a normal woman when she was all grown up. Parents lied to children when they thought it was necessary, or when they thought that it would somehow make things better. It only made sense that children should lie to parents in the same way.

This, then, was Katherine Victoria Lundy: pretty and patient and practical. Not lonely, because she had never really considered any way of being other than alone. Not gregarious, nor sullen, but somewhere in the middle, happy to speak when spoken to, happy also to carry on in silence, keeping her thoughts tucked quietly away. She was ordinary. She was remarkable.

Of such commonplace contradictions are weapons made. Katherine Lundy walked in the world. That was quite enough to set everything else into motion.

2 WHEN IS A DOOR NOT A DOOR?

The school bell rang loud and lofty across the campus, and the doors of the classrooms slammed open in euphonious unison as children boiled forth, clutching their schoolbags and their report cards in their hands, racing for the exits like they feared summer would be canceled if they dawdled too long. The teachers, who would normally have been demanding that they slow down, no running in the halls, indulgently watched them go. Some of it may have been the memory of their own school days, their own golden afternoons when the summer stretched ahead of them in an eternity of opportunity; some of it may simply have been exhaustion. It had been a long school year. They looked forward to the break as much as the children did.

In some classrooms, however, the teachers were looking at the students who *hadn't* bolted for the door. The ones who couldn't, due to braces on their legs or canes in their hands, who took more time to make the same journeys; the ones who were packing up their desks with exquisite slowness, giving their personal demons time to make their way off campus and into the hazy light of summer. And, in Miss Hansard's second-grade classroom, the one who was still tucked in at her desk, peacefully reading.

"Katherine," said Miss Hansard.

Katherine ignored her. Not maliciously: Katherine frequently didn't hear her name the first time it was called, preferring to keep her nose in her book and continue whatever adventure she had decided was more interesting than the actual world around her.

Miss Hansard cleared her throat. *"Katherine,"* she said again, more firmly. She didn't want to yell at the girl, Heaven knew; no one ever wanted to yell at the girl. If anything, she was grateful that Katherine was a pleasant, tractable bookworm, and not a hellion like her older brother. Teachers who found Daniel Lundy assigned to their classrooms frequently found themselves considering how nice it would be to retire early.

Katherine raised her head, blinking owlishly. "Yes, Miss Hansard?" she asked.

"The bell rang. You're free to go." When Katherine still didn't spring from her seat and race for the door, Miss Hansard clarified, "It's summer vacation. School is over for the year."

"Yes, Miss Hansard," said Katherine obediently. She bent her head back over her book.

Miss Hansard counted to ten before she said,

somewhat annoyed, "I would like to lock my classroom and go home, Katherine. That means you have to leave." In all her years of teaching, she had encountered every manner of slothful student—the lazy, the confused, the fearful—but she had never before encountered a student who simply refused to go when the final bell rang.

"My father can lock up when he comes to collect me," said Katherine.

Miss Hansard paused. It was tempting to take the girl at her word—and since no one had ever caught Katherine in an actual *lie,* it would have been understandable for her to do so. Katherine didn't lie; her father was the principal; her father was coming to collect her. It was an easy chain. Unfortunately, there was a piece missing.

"Is your father expecting to come and collect you from my classroom?" asked Miss Hansard. "It would have been polite of him to inform me, if so."

"No, Miss Hansard," said Katherine regretfully. She hunched her shoulders, reading faster.

Miss Hansard sighed. "So you simply assumed he would see the light on and find you here, at which time he would lock up, and I would get a disciplinary note for leaving one of my students unattended."

Katherine said nothing.

"Up, please, Katherine. It's time for you to go."

Knowing when she was beaten, Katherine

slouched to her feet, tucking her book into her bag, and started for the door. Miss Hansard sighed as she watched her go. Katherine really was an excellent student. A little reserved, and a little overly fond of looking for loopholes, but still, an excellent student.

"Katherine," she called.

"Yes, Miss Hansard?"

"You were a joy to teach. Whoever has that opportunity next year will be very lucky."

Katherine seemed to mull her words over for a while, considering them from every angle. Then she smiled. "Thank you, Miss Hansard," she said, and slipped out, leaving the classroom suddenly, echoingly empty.

Miss Hansard, who had been teaching for nearly twenty years, slumped against her desk and wondered when retirement had gone from a distant impossibility to something to be devoutly yearned for. They got younger every year. She was certain of that much, at least. They got younger, and harder to understand, every single year.

The other students were gone, whirling off into the dawning summer like dandelion seeds in the wind. Katherine looked mournfully back at the classroom once before she started walking away. It would have been nice to spend a little longer at her desk, reading where no one knew how to find her. As soon as she got home, her mother would probably try to pass Diana off to her for "just a few minutes, be a good girl now and help your mother," and that would mean playing babysitter for the rest of the afternoon. She didn't particularly want to go outside and run around playing the sort of games that weren't safe for toddlers, but she didn't want to be stuck keeping Diana from eating thumbtacks, either.

Daniel never had to babysit. Daniel could have spent all day, every day reading in his room if he'd wanted to, and their parents would have been right there to applaud and tell him how amazing he was for being so serious about his studies. They didn't discourage her, exactly, didn't tell her she wasn't supposed to read because she was a girl or that she needed to be better at her chores, but there was always a vague impression that they expected something different from her, and she didn't know what to do with that. She didn't *want* to know what to do with that. She suspected it would involve changing everything about who she was, and she liked who she was. It was familiar.

Dwelling on what would happen when she got home made her uncomfortable. She took her book back out of her bag and began to read, following Trixie Belden and her friends into another mystery. Mysteries in books were the best kind. The real world was absolutely full of boring mysteries, questions that never got answered and lost things that never got found. That wasn't allowed, in books. In books, mysteries were always interesting and exciting, packed with daring and danger, and in the end, the good guys found the clues and the bad guys got their comeuppance. Best of all, nothing was ever lost forever. If something mattered enough for the author to write it down, it would come back before the last page was turned. It would always come back.

Katherine had made the walk home from school hundreds of times, tagging at her brother's heels when she was in kindergarten, forging her own trail in first grade, and now following it with the faithful devotion of one who knows the way. She didn't look up as she walked, allowing her feet to remember where they needed to fall if she was going to be home before dark.

It is an interesting thing, to trust one's feet. The heart may yearn for adventure while the head thinks sensibly of home, but the feet are a mixture of the two, dipping first one way and then the other. Katherine's feet were as sensible as the rest of her, trained into obedience by day after day of walking the same path, following the same commands. They knew where to go, and needed no input from her eyes. So it was truly an act of unthinkable rebellion when, at the corner of Pine and Sycamore, her feet—acting entirely on their own—turned left instead of right.

At first Katherine, deeply engrossed in her book and trusting in the inalienability of routine, didn't notice the deviation. She continued walking as the familiar streets dropped farther and farther behind her, replaced first by the shabby neighborhood which bordered the creek, and then by an old walking trail that wound its way through a field of blackberry brambles. It was only when a shadow fell across her book, rendering it temporarily impossible to read, that she stopped and looked up, blinking at the unexpected absence of light.

In front of her, growing right in the middle of the path, was a tree.

Now, while this path was not a customary part of her journey home—was, in fact, some distance from any route she should have been taking—she had walked on it before, picking blackberries in the summer or using it as a shortcut to the local library. And there had never, on any of her journeys, been a tree there.

Katherine looked at the tree. The tree, so far as she could know or tell, did not look back, having no eyes to speak of. It was a good tree, the kind with branches that begged to be climbed and bark that should have been scarred with a dozen sets of initials, summer romances preserved for eternity in the body of a living thing. Its trunk was not a straight upward progression, but rather a long meander, a crooked line stretching from root to crown. She could not have closed her arms around it had she tried. Three girls her size couldn't have accomplished that particular feat.

Its branches, which were thick and dense enough to block a remarkable amount of sunlight, were covered in leaves spanning the entire spectrum of green, from a pale shade that verged on soapy white all the way to a color that stopped barely shy of black. None of them seemed to be quite the same shape as its neighbors. It was a patchwork, an impossible thing. Katherine took a step back.

"What kind of tree *are* you?" she asked—for, as a child who spent the greatest part of her time in comfortable, unchallenging solitude, she had never quite lost the habit of speaking to herself when there was no one else around to talk to.

Had the tree responded with words, this would have been a very brief tale. Katherine, being a sensible girl, would have screamed and run for home, and never again allowed her feet to follow an uncharted trail into the fringes of mystery. She would have grown up stolid and silent, and found the husband she had once believed the world would conjure for her, and become the librarian she had always wanted to be. Her own children might have been more adventurous in their day, for it sometimes seems as if adventure can skip a generation, choosing to remain unpredictable and hence unchained.

Yes, had the tree responded with words, we would be finished now, and all the things which are set to follow would never have come to pass. Perhaps that would, in a way, have been the kinder outcome. Perhaps it would have spared a few broken hearts, a few shattered dreams. But the tree, which had been asked that same question before, did not reply aloud. Instead, the trunk *twisted,* like a washcloth being slowly wrung dry by an unseen hand, and a door worked its way into view while Katherine stared with wide and disbelieving eyes.

Her book fell from her suddenly nerveless fingers, landing in the dust of the trail. This will be important later.

The door in the tree was neither large nor ornate, but barely big enough for a child of her size to climb through, should she choose to do so. The hinges, the frame, even the doorknob, all were made of wood, stripped of its bark and gleaming pale as bone in the thin summer sunlight which filtered down through the branches. At the center of the door, exactly where her eyeline fell, someone had carved a square made of branches and vines, blackberry for the bottom, grape for the sides, and pomegranate for the top. All of them dripped with heavy, wooden fruit, at once crude and so realistically rendered that her mouth watered with a sudden, inexplicable hunger.

Inside the square, surrounded by fruit and

contained by the graven border, were two words: BE SURE.

"Be sure of what?" asked Katherine, who would have run had the tree chosen to speak, but who was still a child, after all, and an imaginative, remarkable child beside. The movement of the tree had not startled her as it would have an adult. The world was filled with things she did not quite understand, and she knew that plants could move: the progress of the zucchini across her mother's garden proved that. So who was to say that a tree might not move, if given the right motivation?

That *she* should be the right motivation was flattering, in a deep-down, inexplicable way. She had never really considered herself to be worth that sort of attention.

The tree didn't move again. The door didn't open. It remained exactly as it was, tantalizing and strange, with those two little words—be sure? Be sure of what? She was sure of her skin, of her self, of her name, but somehow she didn't think that was what the tree intended—hanging in front of her eyes, an unanswered question that contained absolutely everything.

Katherine took a step forward, one hand reaching thoughtlessly outward, until her outstretched fingertips were barely an inch from the wood. The carved fruits seemed to shimmer, like they had been coated in a thin layer of dew.

She wanted to touch them more than she wanted anything else in the world . . . and so she did, brushing her hand across the image, feeling the soft warmth left by the summer sun. The shimmer remained, but the wood itself was dry as a bone.

Again, had she been older, Katherine might have seen this for a warning. Wood does not customarily glitter. Few things do, unless they are attempting to lure something closer to themselves. Sparkle and shine are pleasures reserved for predators, who can afford the risk of courting attention. The exceptions—which exist, for all things must have exceptions—are almost entirely poisonous, and will sicken whatever they lure. So even the exception feeds into the rule, which states that a bright, shimmering thing is almost certainly looking to be seen, and that which hopes to be seen is pursuing its own agenda.

The doorknob turned, entirely on its own. Not all the way, not enough to undo a latch or open a door, but . . . it turned all the same, a little half-twist that drew Katherine's eyes away from the carving and down toward the motion. If the doorknob could turn, it wasn't locked, she realized.

The door could be opened.

No sooner had the thought formed than it became the most important thing she had ever considered. The door, the mysterious door with

33

its mysterious admonition, could be *opened*. She could open it, and see what was on the other side. Why, perhaps she could even meet the person who had instructed her to be sure, and tell them that she was Katherine Lundy, she was *always* sure, no matter what. Hadn't she survived four whole years of school without any friends? Couldn't she read faster than anyone else she knew? She was *always* sure.

The only thing she wasn't sure of was why she was hesitating. She looked at the words again, etched deep into the wood. This was no pocketknife carving, done by one of the tough teenagers from the high school on the other side of town. This was beautiful. Her mother would have been happy to hang something that beautiful in the hall, and her father wouldn't have sniffed when he saw it, rejecting it as a childish art project. This was *real,* in a hard-edged, intangible way she didn't have the vocabulary to articulate, but understood all the same.

Be sure. She only had one chance to decide whether or not she was. She knew that. She didn't know how she knew, but she knew all the same.

"I *am* sure," she said, and grasped the knob. It spun in her hand, eager to fulfill its purpose, and the door swung open, soft white light flooding out into the shadows beneath the tree. Katherine stepped through. The door slammed shut behind her.

For a moment, everything on the trail remained the same. Then, like a patch of dust being broken up by the wind, the tree began to fade away, turning golden as the sunlight that lanced through its now-insubstantial branches. The solid wood dissolved into tiny dancing motes of light, until those too were gone, and only the ordinary, unblocked trail remained.

The trail, and *Trixie Belden and the Black Jacket Mystery*, which had fallen facedown in the dirt, forgotten in the face of a greater mystery.

It would be several hours before the Lundys realized Katherine wasn't holed up in her room, reading and hoping to avoid her chores. It would be another hour after that before Daniel returned from his survey of her usual hiding spots—the creek, the trees behind the school, the swing set at the local park—and reported that she was nowhere to be found. The police would be called, the town would be alerted, and sometime after that, the book would be found, opened, identified as hers. The search would begin.

But not yet. Here and now, there was only the trail, the book, and the absence of the tree.

Everything else would come later.

3 RULES ARE RULES, NO EXCEPTIONS, NO APPEAL

Katherine stepped through the impossible door into the tree and found herself in a long, curving hallway that looked as if it had been carved from a single piece of wood. There were no corners where the walls met the floor or ceiling: instead, a soft curve helped each blend into the next, smoothly wiping away all distinctions. Everything was golden and pale, polished to a gleaming sheen and striated with the wavy lines she had seen in other pieces of cut wood.

A long rug patterned in a beautiful blend of grapevines and blackberry creepers stretched from where she stood into the unseen distance, keeping her feet from slipping on the slick floor. It was softly worn, as if many feet had walked on it before she came.

Her eyes widened. This was someone's *house*. It had to be. Hallways and rugs weren't the sort of things one found inside trees; they belonged in houses, where they were loved and cleaned and cared for by the people who owned them. Which meant she was *trespassing*. And trespassing was *against the rules*.

Katherine understood rules. Understood them down to the marrow of her bones. Rules were the reason the world could work at all. Following the rules didn't make you a good person, just like breaking them didn't make you a bad one, but it could make you an invisible person, and invisible people got to do as they liked. She never, *never* broke the rules if there was any way to avoid it, and when she did break them—say, by trespassing in a stranger's house just because that stranger happened to live inside a tree—she stopped as quickly as she could.

She whirled and reached for the doorknob, intending to let herself out before anyone had time to realize she was there . . . only the door was gone, replaced by more hallway, stretching out for what felt like forever. Katherine froze.

Trees didn't suddenly appear where they hadn't been before. People didn't make their houses entirely out of a single piece of wood. Doors didn't disappear as soon as they were used. The number of things that didn't happen but were happening anyway seemed to be piling up, and up, and up, until it felt like they should be scraping against the sky.

For maybe the first time since her sixth birthday, when she had decided she didn't need anyone who didn't need her, Katherine was unsure.

This did not make the door reappear.

"Oh," she said softly. The hallway swallowed

the sound, making it something small and meek and forgettable. She didn't like that, and so she said again, "Oh," louder this time, trying to sound surprised, like she had no idea how she had come to be in this place where she wasn't supposed to be, where she couldn't *possibly* be, since there wasn't any door.

No one came to ask her why she was in their hallway, or show her the way out. Katherine frowned. This was going to take a little more effort than simple surprise.

The door wasn't there: more hallway was. Walking that way should have been impossible, meaning it was against the rules in some intangible, difficult-to-articulate way. Katherine turned again, until she was facing the way she had been originally. Despite having no visible lights at all, the hall was quite well lit, as bright as her bedroom when she plugged her nightlight in. She could almost have read a book without—

Her hand clenched. Her book was gone. She dimly remembered dropping it when confronted with the impossible tree. She didn't remember picking it up again. Her frown became a scowl. Books were precious things, meant to be treated well, both because they deserved it and because if she didn't treat them well, her parents might stop buying them for her. Leaving them lying in the dirt while she ran off to impossible places certainly didn't count as treating them *well*.

Nothing to be done about it now, except for getting out of here as soon as she could. She took a step forward before glancing back over her shoulder. The door did not take her movement as a reason to reappear. Sighing, Katherine looked resolutely down the hall and started walking.

Like the tree trunk, the hall was not perfectly straight: it bent and twisted, slowly, by degrees, until she could have been walking in a circle without properly realizing it. The light grew brighter as she walked, going from nightlight to hallway light to proper overhead light. This, she could read by.

No sooner had the thought formed than the first of the frames appeared on the wall. It contained a cross-stitch, neatly done, with an embroidered marigold in one corner. Katherine stopped.

" 'Rule one,' " she read. " 'Ask for nothing.' How funny that is! Although maybe that means I'm not allowed to ask for the way out? I've never heard of a rule like that before."

She resumed walking, and shortly came upon a second frame. Again, she stopped.

" 'Rule two,' " she read. " 'Names have power.' What does that even *mean?*"

The walls did not reply. Katherine walked on, faster now, hurrying to find the next sign.

Rule three was "always give fair value." Rule four was "take what is offered and be grateful." And rule five, most puzzling of all, was, "remember the curfew."

"None of this makes any *sense,*" she complained, and heard a soft click, as of a door latch coming open. She turned. There, on the hallway wall, which she was sure had been smooth and featureless only a moment before, was a door. It was standing ajar, tempting her to come and see what might be waiting on the other side. She bit her lip, lightly, staring at it.

If the door was open, surely that was an invitation to go through it, wasn't it? And she was already trespassing. It wasn't like going through an open, unlocked door would mean she was trespassing *more.*

Carefully, Katherine approached the door. It didn't disappear, which had never been a concern before, but was now an all-consuming one. She nudged it with her toe. It swung a little farther open, and something new appeared: a beam of light too buttery and bright to be artificial. Sunlight. She had found the exit. She wasn't going to get in trouble after all. Beaming, Katherine shoved the door open and stepped through, emerging, not into the fields along the path or even into the well-maintained yard of some stranger's house, but into a dream. She stopped, trying to stare in every direction at once, until it felt like her eyes were going to cross in her head with the effort of taking it all in.

If a carnival and a farmer's market and a craft fair all decided to happen at the same time, in the same field, the result might have been something like what was in front of her. Everywhere she looked there were tents, and painted wagons, and little stalls with fabric walls and decorated awnings. Pens filled with animals—goats and chickens and pigs—stood side by side with rickety cases packed tight with leather-bound books whose spines glittered with gold leaf and what she thought might be real rubies. Figures moved by with sacks slung over their shoulders and yokes across their necks, the ends weighted down with buckets filled with mushrooms, or potatoes, or water that rippled from the motion of impossible fish.

Figures, not people: she wasn't sure the word "people" was big enough to encompass everything she was seeing. Some of them were no bigger than her hand, soaring along on green moth's wings, their hair like candle flames that flickered in the sunlight. Others were so big she could have mistaken them for boulders, with skin as gray as granite and hands almost as large as her body. It was like there was some sort of spectrum, and she was right smack in the middle, neither big nor small, neither fair nor foul.

A few of the figures moving by without giving her so much as a glance looked like they might have been human, and somehow they were the worst of all, because if they were human, this was really happening, and if this was really happening, then the rules she had known for her whole life were wrong. None of these things were covered. If nothing here was real, she was safe, but if any of it really existed . . .

"First time, huh?"

Katherine whirled and found herself eye to eye with a girl of her own height, with pale, dirty skin and small brown feathers tied in her long brown hair. The feathers only held Katherine's attention for a moment before it switched, inevitably, to the girl's *eyes*. They had no whites. The girl's pupils were too big, surrounded by a dark orange iris that extended from corner to corner, lid to lid. Katherine did what was, under the circumstances, the only reasonable thing to do. She screamed.

A few of the passing strangers looked over with vague interest, taking in the pair of them without slowing their strides. The girl with the feathers in her hair rolled her impossible eyes, which somehow made them seem even larger, and more orange.

"You shouldn't make so much noise," said the girl, peevishly. "You'll attract attention, and I don't feel like putting on a panto right now, do you?" Her accent was plummy and strange, all out of keeping with her tatterdemalion appearance.

Tatterdemalion. That was a good word. Katherine seized on to it, trying to smother her screams with intellectual curiosity. She had known the word for months, of course, had learnt it in a book she was supposed to be too young to read, but this was the first time she'd seen someone who looked like it could apply to them.

The owl-eyed girl was wearing a patchwork vest bedecked with odd strips of ribbon and fringe over a cream-colored shirt in some rough fabric, with sleeves that had once been longer, before they'd been hacked off just below the shoulders. Her pants were funny, made of dark brown canvas with bright patches on the knees and cuffs, too tight to be fashionable, too short to fit right. She had no shoes, and her toenails were the longest and thickest Katherine had ever seen.

"What's a panto?" asked Katherine.

"A pantomime, a performance, a *play*," said the girl, looking pleased that Katherine was doing something other than screaming. "If we attract too much attention we'll need to give fair value for it, and that means a performance or a promise. I don't have any promises in me this week, and you're so new you still have that new-penny smell all around you. You shouldn't be making any promises until you know what they mean, and that's going to take someone explaining the rules to you."

Katherine hesitated. "Someone like you?"

The girl's eyes widened with alarm. "No! No-no-no, someone *not* like me! I'm not equipped for teaching someone how to give fair value, I mean, *look* at me." She spread her hands, which were long-fingered and slim, indicating the sweep of her body. "If I told you what to do you'd wind up in the same boat I'm in, and it's not a very big boat. Put two of us here and we might sink. No, no, I'll leave the explaining to the Archivist. But you should come with me, and you should stop asking questions, before you ask the kind of thing with an answer that doesn't come free."

"Where am—"

Before Katherine could finish the sentence, the owl-eyed girl was standing nose to nose with her, one hand clasped across Katherine's mouth. Her skin smelled like cinnamon, underscored with a sharp, unfamiliar herbal note.

"You were about to ask where you were, even though I just told you to stop asking questions," said the owl-eyed girl. Her voice was low, pleasant, and somehow dangerous. "You were going to keep going, and going, and dig a debt to bury yourself in. Be *quiet*. Didn't you see the rules when you came through the passage? Didn't you *read?* You can be happy here or you wouldn't be here. But 'happy' doesn't mean the rules don't apply to you."

Katherine stared at her.

"I'm going to take my hand away. You're not going to ask any more questions. You're going to follow me to the Archivist, and *she* can tell you what 'fair value' means, and we can be friends, you and me, if you want to be. All right?" The owl-eyed girl nodded firmly. "All right. I'm letting go now."

She did. Katherine took a step backward, out of reach, although she knew it wouldn't do her any good: the girl had moved so swiftly and silently that there had been no evading her. "I didn't say you could touch me," she said, and her voice was shrill, edged with panic. "I want to go now."

The impossible people were still passing, the impossible tents and stalls and wagons were still there, and the air smelled like barbequing meat and sticky fruit pies and this was wrong, this was *wrong,* this couldn't be *happening—*

"Good," said the owl-eyed girl brightly. "Let's go." She grabbed Katherine's hand and dove into the crowd, dragging Katherine in her wake. Too surprised to struggle, Katherine found herself darting and weaving between the strange figures, most of whom spared the two girls little more than a glance. This sort of thing was apparently commonplace here.

What Katherine had *meant* was that she wanted to go home, back to a world where things made sense and girls with orange eyes didn't touch her without permission. But she hadn't said that, had she? She'd said she wanted to go, and they were going. It was a loophole, one she'd created with her own voice, and she grudgingly respected it, even as she allowed herself to be pulled along.

After a few seconds, she relaxed and started looking around, letting the owl-eyed girl lead the way. There was so much to see, so much to hear and smell and take note of to remember later. Not all the smells were pleasant ones—livestock and too many bodies saw to that—but there were more spices and sweet fruits than garbage piles and outhouses. A rooster crew in the distance. Someone played a fiddle, the tune dancing rapidly from one key to another, climbing like a boy in a fairy tale climbed a beanstalk.

Yes. That was the answer, and Katherine seized on it with both hands. If she thought of this as a fairy tale that she had somehow stumbled into, she could handle it. She knew the rules of fairy tales. Most importantly of all, she knew that fairy tales ended with "happy ever after" and everything being just fine. Better than fine: with everything being perfect. Perfect would be all right. She liked the idea of perfect.

The owl-eyed girl ran until the crowd began to thin around them, until they were past the wagons and the tents and the stalls. She ran until the sounds of people passing were replaced by the warble and caw and screech of birds, until the branches of the trees that were closing in around them—big trees, climbing trees, patchwork trees that looked suspiciously like the one where the door had been—dripped with birdcages instead of fruit. They were filled with birds the likes of

which Katherine had never seen before, birds in every color of the rainbow and a few the rainbow itself had forgotten about. The ones she *did* recognize seemed bigger and cleverer than the ones she knew, pigeons the size of chickens, eagles with wings whose span must have been measured in exclamations instead of inches.

Somewhere on their journey through the impossible market, they had stepped onto a narrow ribbon of a path that wound and twisted through those bird-laden trees. At its end was a house. Katherine supposed it was a house, at least; it could also have been called a hut, if she was being charitable, and a shack, if she wasn't. It was too small to be more than one room no bigger than her own, with mossy shingles on the roof and bright geometric designs painted on the walls. A porch ran all the way around it, groaning under the weight of the container gardens stacked from wall to edge, each of them brimming with herbs.

The owl-eyed girl came to a sudden stop a few feet from the door, dragging Katherine to a halt. Katherine stumbled, glaring at the owl-eyed girl, who didn't seem to notice. Instead, she dropped Katherine's hand in order to cup her own hands around her mouth.

"Hello, the house!" she shouted. "It's Moon! I'm outside! I found a new girl! She doesn't know the rules!"

"I read them," said Katherine peevishly. "One of

them was 'names have power.' Should you really be shouting your name like it isn't anything?"

"That isn't my name, new girl," said the owl-eyed girl. She *did* look like someone who could be called "Moon" without anyone laughing at her. Her face was narrow and her cheeks were flushed, but there was something about her that spoke of midnights and secrets and things no one dared to say during the day. "That's just what people say when they want to talk about me. Whatever your name is, you don't give it to anyone you meet here. Promise me."

"I don't—"

Once again, Moon was in her face too fast and too silently to have been seen in motion. It was like she'd foregone one place for another without traveling the distance between. "*Promise* me," she hissed. "Your name is your heart, and you don't give your heart away. *Promise.*"

"I promise," said Katherine, wide eyed and suddenly, inexplicably afraid.

"Good." Moon stepped back.

The door swung open. A woman stepped out.

She was tall. Taller than Katherine or Moon; taller even than Katherine's father, who was the yardstick she used to measure out the world. Her hair was the color of freshly grated cinnamon, and her skin was the pleasant brown of a sparrow's feathers. She wore a long white dress with a red shawl tied around her shoulders, and she was beautiful, and she was terrible, and Katherine couldn't decide whether she wanted to love her or leave her as fast as she could.

She walked toward the two girls, head cocked gently to the side as she took them in. "Who have you brought me, Moon?" she asked, and her voice was rough, rough as granite, rough as the bark of a tree.

"I don't have her name and she knows better than to give it," said Moon. Turning to Katherine, she said, "This is the Archivist. That's not her name, either, but she knows the rules better than anybody, and she's allowed to teach them to you, if you come to her without a debt on you. I saw you come and you'll see me go, and you're free and clear. Ask her what you need to know."

"The first rule was 'ask for nothing,' " said Katherine. Her body felt heavy, like she was wrapped in fog. It was becoming harder and harder to dismiss this as a dream, and if it wasn't a dream, it was really happening, and if it was really happening, she was standing and talking to people who called themselves "Moon" and "the Archivist," and she was *awfully* far from home.

"I waive the first rule for the duration of this conversation and no further," said the Archivist. "There will be no debt incurred by any questions you may ask: the only fair value I need is your understanding, so that your future debts will not come to darken my door. Moon, you may go."

"Don't need to tell me twice," said Moon. She tipped a wink at Katherine. "See you around, new girl." Then she was gone, running off into the trees with that preternatural speed, disappearing among the branches and the birds.

"Come with me," said the Archivist, and offered Katherine her hand.

Lacking any other choice, Katherine took it. The Archivist led her into the house, as the birds in their cages shrieked and sang their mournful, captive songs.

4 FAIR VALUE

The inside of the Archivist's house was as small as the outside, which came as something of a relief to Katherine, who had already encountered one major violation of the laws of physics since school let out, and wasn't sure she could handle another one so soon. Every surface that could be commandeered to hold a bookshelf had been, and every shelf was packed to the point of bursting. Stacks of books covered the floor, too numerous to be contained. The only other furniture was a small wooden table with spindly legs and two matching chairs, tucked into the far corner of the room.

"Come," said the Archivist, and walked to the table, settling herself in one of the chairs. She gestured to the other. "Sit."

Katherine sat. The chair groaned under her weight, slight as it was. She thought the Archivist must have been the lightest person in the world to sit so comfortably on something so breakable.

"This is my home, and you are safe here, for now," said the Archivist, in a calm, clear voice. "Do you know your name?"

Katherine started to answer. Then she caught herself, remembering her promise to Moon. She closed her mouth and nodded.

"Excellent," said the Archivist. "Keep knowing it. If you forget or lose your name, you do the same to your self, and there are consequences for such things. But you'll need a name you can use here, something that lacks the teeth of the name you wear every day. Something you'll answer to that's harder to use against you. It could be an attribute, or a thing you like very much, or a family name that isn't exclusively yours. I can choose one for you, if you'd like."

"Lundy," said Katherine.

"Lundy." The Archivist cocked her head again. "You're not the first of that name to wander here. I can see him in the corners of your eyes. Welcome, Lundy, to the Goblin Market."

Katherine—Lundy—who had never considered that her father must have been young once, might have gone on adventures of his own, frowned. "What's the Goblin Market?"

"It is a place where dreamers go when they don't fit in with the dreams their homes think worth dreaming. Doors lead here. Perhaps you found one."

Lundy bit her lip, and said nothing.

"We began with a single peddler's son who lost his way. He decided to set up camp and wait for his mother to come back. She didn't. He found me, instead, and we were happy, for a time. But others came after him, and others after them, until we had a community. Until we needed rules—and borders, of a kind, since our doors are the type that may open a dozen times for the same person, rather than only once." The Archivist leaned forward. Her face was kind. "Did you see the rules, when you came through the passage?"

"Yes," said Lundy. Then, in a rush, "But I didn't understand them. How can I follow them if I don't *understand* them?"

"A complicated question, to be sure, especially since the rules have a way of enforcing themselves. Moon pays some of her debts through me by watching for children like you. She wasn't careful when she first started needing to provide fair value—she got here too young, and spent too long in a state of grace to understand what consequences were."

"What happens if you don't provide fair value?"

"Nothing you'd care to experience. Now. We've covered the second rule, but not the first. While you are here, you must ask for nothing. Work around the question. If you desire a drink of water, don't say 'may I have some water,' say 'I would like some water,' or 'I'm thirsty.' Be prepared to hear a price quoted in return. It will take you a while to decide which prices are fair, so ask yourself, every time, whether the water is worth the loss of a sock, or a strand of hair, or a secret. One of those is fair value."

"The sock?" guessed Lundy.

"The hair," said the Archivist. "A strand isn't enough to do anything to you, and some people enjoy weaving with it. Socks, unless you have a very strange schoolbag, only come two to a person, and your feet will get cold."

It was a refreshingly logical way of looking at things. Lundy nodded. "What happens if I ask for something?"

"The way you're doing now? Don't look so alarmed; I gave you permission. If you ask outside this house, anyone you talk to could decide that you're offering them a purchase, and once you've asked directly, it's not a negotiation. Do you understand? Say 'can I have a glass of water' and I can say 'that will be one sock,' and if you don't pay, you've broken rule three. You haven't given fair value. Debt will follow."

"What does debt mean, if you don't pay for things with money?"

The Archivist pursed her lips. "You'll learn soon enough, little girl. When someone offers you something free of charge—as I'm doing now—you follow rule four. You take it, and you be grateful, because something that is free for you may be very expensive for someone else. People will remember if you're not grateful. People will stop offering."

Lundy nodded slowly. "All right."

"There is one more rule you must follow. It won't seem very important to you right now, but you need to mind it anyway, for it's the rule that can do you true and lasting harm if you're not careful." The Archivist leaned forward. "Do you remember what it was? Did you see it in the passage?"

"Um . . . 'remember the curfew,'" said Lundy, dutiful and dubious at the same time.

"Yes," said the Archivist. "There is a curfew, Lundy, and it comes for all of us. It's not the kind of curfew you may know. It doesn't mean 'all good little children come inside at sundown.' It means we must be sure no one is trapped here against their will. It means we want all those who crave citizenship in our admittedly unusual land to have chosen their way with care. The doors have found you now. They will open for you again and again, and you can take them or you can walk away, until the day you turn eighteen. On that day, arbitrary as it might seem, the doors will close. If you've kept fair value in mind, when you turn eighteen, you'll be allowed to choose which side of the door you stand on. If you haven't—if you're too deeply in debt to one person or another—you won't be allowed to stand on the side of the door you come from. It may seem unfair, but it's necessary. Fair value says we don't steal what isn't ours. It also says that what we own, we keep."

"I don't understand," said Lundy.

"Understanding is something that comes with time, I'm afraid, no matter how clearly we try to explain," said the Archivist. "There are many good things here, Lundy. Many wonderful things. You could be happy here, if you wanted to be. But you don't have forever to decide, and you must follow the rules, or you'll surely pay the price."

Lundy frowned. "Does this mean I don't get to go home?" she asked, finally.

"You must not be *too* attached to your home, or you would never have found us in the first place," said the Archivist. "But no. That isn't what this means. You'll be here for a time, and then you'll find a door, and you'll be able to return to the world you left. No one stays forever on their first visit. How could they? One visit isn't long enough to be sure. The rules mean—only—that once your eighteenth birthday comes, there will be no more doors. For now, you have the freedom of the Market. Remember the rules. Try not to break them, unless you feel like paying the price. Enjoy yourself. There are many good things in the world, and each of them happens for the first time only once, and never again. Do you understand?"

Lundy, who didn't understand, but who had long since learned that adults were happier when they thought she needed no more guidance, nodded. "Can I come back here when you're not teaching me?" she asked. "Only, you have *so* many books, and I love to read."

Adults also loved a scholarly child. The Archivist blinked once before she smiled, warm and suddenly accepting. "I would be happy to let you read my books, and the only price I would ask is that you treat them kindly, and tell me what you think of their contents."

Book reports were something Lundy had a great deal of experience with. "That seems like, um, fair value," she said.

The Archivist's smile broadened. "You're getting it already," she said. "Run along and play now. Moon can show you the places children like to go, and I'll let some of the others know that you've come. The rules apply from the moment you arrive, but we can choose to interpret them as generously as possible during your first visit, to make it easier for you to make a second one. Run along, now. See what the Goblin Market can offer you."

Lundy, who was not a fool, jumped off her rickety chair and dipped an impulsive curtsey before running to the door and out, into the clear, smoke-scented air. A raucous chorus of screams and warbles greeted her as the birds in the surrounding branches cried out, marking her arrival. She stopped to frown at one big pied crow.

60

"Nobody gets to sneak around here, do they?" she asked.

"Some of us do," said a voice at her shoulder.

Lundy shouted and jumped into the air, spinning around to find Moon standing behind her. The other girl had a small, smug smile on her lips, and her odd orange eyes were half closed, making her look sleepy and overly pleased with herself.

"The birds don't scream when they see me," she said. "They *remember*. You all done with the Archivist? Did she teach you everything you need to know?"

"I thought we weren't supposed to ask questions," said Lundy.

"You asked a question just a few seconds ago," said Moon. "Some questions are okay. You can't have people without questions. People are too curious for that, they'd get all gummed up and stop working right if you didn't let them have questions once in a while. But there's a big difference between asking for things and only asking. 'Do you think there will be grapes sometime this week' isn't the same as 'can I have some of those grapes.' Do you understand?"

"No," said Lundy sullenly.

"Then I guess you'll have to do like the rest of us do, and figure it out as you go along." Moon suddenly, impulsively seized her hands, orange

61

eyes wide and bright. "I can help. I can take three debts for you, if you promise you'll take them back from me if I ever need you to."

"What?"

"Debts. When you don't give fair value, you get debts. But you're a first-timer, you don't know how careful feels yet. So I can go with you, and if you get any debts, I can take three of them on your behalf. That's allowed. Then, if I ever need it, you'll agree to take them back, right? Once you know what you're doing."

"That seems fair," said Lundy slowly. She wasn't actually certain that it did, but she couldn't see a way around it that wasn't cruel to the other girl.

"Shake on it." Moon stuck out one long-fingered hand. "Come on. Shake."

Lundy shook. Moon beamed.

"Come on," she said. "I'll show you the Market." She took off running and Lundy, not knowing what else to do, followed.

They ran through the golden afternoon like dandelion seeds dancing on the wind, two little girls with all the world in front of them, a priceless treasure ready to be pillaged. Moon was fast and light on her feet, sometimes looping back to circle around Lundy as they both ran, laughing at her companion's slowness. Lundy tensed the first time she heard that laughter, but relaxed as she realized there was no meanness in it, no cruelty; Moon was *playing* with her.

She couldn't think of the last time someone had thought she was worth playing with.

They ran all the way back to the impossible aisles of tents and stalls and wagons, and they kept running, Moon weaving around the shoppers and stall keepers, Lundy struggling to keep up. There were children in the Market, some of them manning counters or counting out apples, while others watched them longingly, tied to their posts with ribbons of silk, or braided steel, or living ivy. A group of boys threw a ball back and forth between them in one of the small open spaces scattered through the rows. They jeered at the girls as they went darting past, but made no effort to stop them.

Moon wasn't the only one with unusual eyes. Some of the children they passed had black eyes, like drops of oil. Others had eyes of yellow, or red, or a startling blue that was more like a fragment of the summer sky than anything that belonged in a human face. Lundy wanted to ask about it, but she wasn't sure whether that would be the safe kind of question or not, and so she kept her mouth closed and her eyes open, drinking in everything around them.

There was a woman in a wheelchair with a shaggy golden dog whose fur flickered around the edges, like it was burning without being consumed. There was a man with four arms, weaving ribbons into beautiful ropes with the speed and ease of a lifetime spent in long practice. There was a centaur of a sort, half human and half unicorn, a single spiraling horn rising from his forehead, taking a tray of meat pies out of an oven large enough to hold an entire bakery.

Lundy's stomach growled. Moon stopped running.

"You must be hungry, you poor thing!" she cried. "That's barely fair value on me, showing you things without stopping to see if you needed. What do you have in your pockets?"

Lundy blinked, thrown by what seemed to be a sudden change of subjects. "What?"

"Your dress. I can see it has pockets. What's *in* them? Anything?" Moon looked hopeful. "Rocks, maybe, or weird coins, or something like that?"

"Um." Lundy reached into her pocket, pulled its contents into the light. "I have two pencils, and a stick of chalk, and a quarter."

"Pencils!" Moon snatched them away before Lundy could protest, tugging her toward the stall where the unicorn was now setting the meat pies on a rack to cool. "Pencils are *gold*. Adults love writing things down. Come on."

She stopped in front of the stall, standing straight and smiling brightly. Lundy glanced at her and imitated her posture, trying not to look as lost as she felt. Everything was a dizzy, confusing whirl of rules and strangeness, and she wanted to go home and she *never* wanted to go home, not until she'd learned everything there was to know about this incredible, impossible place. It was a contradiction so intrinsic that it ached.

Lundy wasn't used to contradictions. She was used to making up her mind and sticking with whatever she decided, to knowing precisely how she was going to proceed from any given point. But she understood rules, and she understood loopholes, and she thought she could learn to enjoy looking for the places where these rules—fair value and not asking questions and all—collided and hence created gaps for her to squeeze through.

The unicorn-centaur frowned. "Moon," he said, dubiously. "What do you want?"

"I have payment," said Moon, holding out her hand to show the pencils she'd snatched from Lundy. "What would fair value be for these?"

The unicorn-centaur's eyes lit up in a way that seemed, to Lundy, entirely out of proportion with the two used, slightly chewed-on pencils. "More than I can spare, if you wanted it all at once. But I'd say ten meat pies and ten fruit pies apiece, delivered whenever you cared to claim them, as long as you promised no more than two of each per day."

"That sounds fair to me," said Moon, and glanced at Lundy.

Lundy sensed the silent question in that look. She nodded, her enthusiasm fueled by the promise of pies. "That sounds like fair value," she agreed.

The unicorn-centaur looked at her measuringly. "New one, aren't you?" he asked.

Lundy nodded again. "Yes, sir."

"Be careful with this one," he said, hooking a thumb in Moon's direction even as he deftly plucked the pencils from her palm. "She's too smart for her own good, and not nearly careful enough for yours."

"Pies, please," said Moon, with a bright grin.

Lundy looked between the two of them. This was a choice that needed to be made, she could tell that much: who to trust was always a choice. But she had already made a bargain with Moon, and she already understood enough about this place to know that she'd be expected to hold up her end of it even if she chose to walk away and not receive the aid she'd been promised.

"Pies, please," she said, with a smile of her own.

The unicorn-centaur rolled his eyes.

Not long after, the two girls were seated under a tree, safely surrounded by other trees that kept them from the view of the market proper, sticky fruit juice on their chins and the crumbs of their meat pies scattered on their laps. The fruit was like nothing Lundy had ever tasted before, sweet and sour and sharp all at the same time, so that every bite was an education. The meat had been equally as good, chicken baked with peas and a delicate cream sauce. The memory was enough to make her mouth water.

"I think we're going to be very good friends," said Moon.

"I've never had a friend before," admitted Lundy shyly. "I don't know if I know how."

Moon beamed. "Don't worry," she said. "I'll teach you, and so will Mockery, and the Archivist, and everyone else who loves me. They're going to love you, too. You'll see."

Lundy smiled back, and thought that the Goblin Market was about the most wonderful place she'd ever been, and she never wanted to go home.

5 A BEGINNING ENDS

Katherine Lundy had been missing for eight days. Long enough that the police were starting to speak in hushed tones of calling off the search: they only had so many resources, after all, and while everyone agreed the girl was too young to have run off on her own, there was a point at which things would need to be turned over to the feds. They had the manpower and the training to pursue a kidnapping across state lines. They could find what the local authorities could not.

At home, her mother wept, her big brother stared sleeplessly out his bedroom window, and her younger sister cried herself fitfully to sleep, unable to quite understand why everyone was so upset, knowing only that her sister—one of the few constants in her life—was gone.

Only her father stayed dry-eyed and steady, standing at the back door, waiting. Even as the police said that they were sorry, they were running out of leads, and would he like to speak to someone higher up, he remained calm. He stood at the door, and he kept his eyes on the horizon, and he thought about a long hallway carved from a single piece of living wood. He thought about rules. They were always so careful with their rules in the Goblin Market. They never kept the children on their first visit. It wouldn't have been fair. They wouldn't have been sure.

He thought about a golden hind with daisies and pomegranate blossoms in her hair, dancing under a midsummer moon. He thought about the way her kisses had burned when she tucked them into the corners of his mouth, telling him to store them up for the rest of his life, to only use them when he absolutely needed to. They had been barely sixteen on that moon-soaked night, and she had already known he was leaving, even though he himself had still believed that he might stay.

He thought about choices—both the one he'd made and the one he knew his daughter was even now making, the choice that would define everything that came after. He had done his best by her, tried to raise her to live in books and quiet, safe rooms, rather than running wild through fields of gorse and heather. He had always assumed that, after Daniel had passed through his elementary school years without stumbling through any impossible doors, the chain had been broken. That it was over.

He had been so wrong. And so he waited, until one evening, as the moon was rising, a bedraggled little figure came walking up the street toward their house.

Katherine's school bag was missing, as were both her socks, and the ribbons from her hair. She had a sharp knife of polished glass belted at her waist, its curved bone handle easy to her hand. She had feathers braided in her hair (and if her father's heart skipped a beat at the sight of them, she wasn't to know why; she didn't yet understand). She had a smudge of fruit juice, dark and sticky as jam, drying on one cheek.

Her father was out the door and down the front steps before her mother even noticed that he was moving, and in less time than it takes to say "home again, home again, she was finally home again," he was on his knees on the sidewalk, holding her close, holding her tight, holding her like the world depended on his never letting go.

Lundy sniffled. Lundy buried her face against the crook of his neck, inhaling that wool and paper and smoke scent that said "father" to her. And Lundy, brave Lundy, who had ridden alongside her friends Moon and Mockery to fight the wicked Wasp Queen for the safety of the pomegranate groves, who had seen that sometimes fair value wasn't enough to prevent blood on the ground and a little girl with silver feathers in her hair lying broken in the leaves, never to mock or tease or mercilessly barter again, burst into tears.

"I'm sorry," she wailed. "I'm sorry, I'm so sorry. I won't go back, I won't."

She was lying, of course. But she wouldn't understand that for two more years.

PART II
WE FIRST MUST SOW

6 BACK THROUGH THE IMPOSSIBLE DOOR

If anyone had asked Katherine Lundy—who was happier these days going by her last name, which no one tried to twist or turn into something shorter, sillier, less tiresome for the tongue—she would have said being ten was substantially harder than being eight, and that she would be perfectly happy to go backward, returning to a time where her femininity had been an attribute rather than an expectation.

At eight, she had been able to wear dresses or tie ribbons in her hair, or both, without anyone pointing to it as proof that she was growing up to be a beautiful little lady. She had been able to raise her hand in class without being skipped over in favor of the boys, whose answers, although often identical to her own, were somehow smarter, more thoughtful, more *necessary*. She had been able to eat sweets without being asked if she was worried about getting fat.

She had been able to find a doorway and disappear into an adventure, instead of living in a world that told her, day after day after grinding, demoralizing day, that adventures were only for boys; that girls had better things to worry about, like making sure those same boys had a safe harbor to come home to.

Now that she was ten, all of the things she'd thought she knew about girls and boys and herself and the people around her were changing. Family friends and distant relations bought her pretty bangles and new hairbrush sets for Christmas, instead of the books and educational toys she had so carefully requested. She supposed the reason girls were told the great secret of Santa Claus was because otherwise they would think the man had quite lost his marbles, to suddenly change the nature of presents that had been perfectly reasonable before.

Her breaking point, when it came, arrived quite abruptly in the middle of her morning math lesson. One of the questions simply *refused* to provide the right answer, no matter how many times she twisted it around. Finally, in frustration, she put her hand up.

"All right, Katie," said her teacher, Mr. Holmen, with a smirk as broad and unwelcome as his mustache. Looking at the rest of the class like he had a secret, he said, "I don't mind giving the girls a little extra help with their math. It doesn't come naturally to them, after all."

All the boys in class snickered. Even Johnny Wells, and *she* had been helping *him* with his math homework all the way since September.

Lundy stood so fast that her math book fell to the floor with a sound like a slap. Mr. Holmen blinked at her, nonplussed.

"I-need-to-go-to-the-bathroom," she said, a single staccato string of syllables with no pauses between them. She didn't wait to be given permission. She turned and fled, running out of the room as fast as she could, leaving her bookbag behind.

She stormed down the hall like it had personally offended her, and somehow it wasn't a surprise when the door to the janitor's closet—a door she walked past every day, several times—was gone. In its place was a tall oak door. A square made of graven fruit and flowers had been carved exactly at her eye level. BE SURE, read the words at its center, and in that moment, Lundy had never been more sure of anything.

"Only wait here a moment," she said politely, eyes on the door. "I need to get my bag." Then she spun on her heel and marched back to the classroom.

Mr. Holmen's head jerked up when she stepped inside. "Detention," he said. "You are not permitted to leave the room without permission."

"I have vomited all over the girls' bathroom," Lundy replied calmly. Some of the other girls looked shocked by this admission. Most of the boys snickered. She didn't care. The wonderful thing about not having any friends was not needing to care what other children thought of her. Let them think that she was crass or rude for being willing to talk about the things her body did—or in this case, didn't do. She was leaving.

She was going home.

"I am going to the office. I will tell my father that I am unwell." Lundy walked to her desk and retrieved her bookbag, watching carefully as Mr. Holmen's cheeks flared red. He hated to be reminded that her father ran the school. Lundy didn't get many special privileges from it—if anything, she was punished more than she was rewarded—but in situations like this one, there was no way to beat a child whose card in the hole was the principal.

"Do you need an escort?" he asked, the words heavy on his tongue, like stones. More of the class giggled, not at the vomiting, but at his loss of face.

"No, thank you," said Lundy. She slung her bag over her shoulder and walked away.

Mr. Holmen would likely be fired when she disappeared, having left his classroom without a hall pass or a helper. Lundy found she didn't care. He shouldn't have treated her like she didn't matter. He shouldn't have treated her like his idea of a *girl*.

The door was still there when she returned to the hall. Lundy smiled, and walked a little faster, until the knob was in her hand and the scent of fresh oak was in her nostrils, and when she stepped through, she felt her anger peel away, shedding it like a snake sheds its skin. The door slammed shut behind her. She didn't bother looking over her shoulder. It was already gone, and so was she.

Once again, the door to the Goblin Market had opened on a tunnel somehow carved into the living body of a tree, and once again, the tunnel ended with an unlocked door, where a single step could carry her from the safety of the passage out into the better, brighter world she had tried so hard to convince herself had been a dream. The mingled odors of a hundred impossible things struck her, and she stopped, breathing in deeply, letting the sounds and sights of the Market surround her, strengthen her, renew her.

For her, it had been two years. It might have been twice as long for the Goblin Market, or it might have been no time at all, from all the changes she could see. Stalls had shifted. A few of the wagons were gone, while a few more had arrived. But the jumble of wares was as wild and unreadable as ever, and the people passing by were as strange as they'd been the first time. Lundy closed her eyes and kept breathing, filling her lungs with the Goblin Market, chasing all traces of school away.

Her stomach rumbled. Lundy opened her eyes,

laughing, and dove into the Market, letting her feet lead the way.

Feet have a longer memory for certain things than minds do, and her feet remembered well the way to get to the pie stall, where Vincent the pie-maker was pulling a tray of sweet fruit pies out of the oven. A rack of lamb pies with baked quince cooled on the counter, next to a dozen butter chicken pies. Lundy's stomach grumbled louder.

"Hello, sir," she said, with surpassing politeness. Even here in the Goblin Market, adults liked it when she was polite and looked tractable. Adults seemed to view mannerly children as somehow superior, and hence deserving of better treatment. It was silly at best and dangerous at worst—some of the nastiest bullies in school were capable of pulling out exquisite manners at the drop of a hat—but it could work for her, when she wanted it to.

Vincent turned, eyes widening fractionally at the sight of her, in her pressed skirt and white school blouse. "You're back," he said. "Moon's tried to claim your share of pies twice, but I told her a deal was a deal, and now it seems I'll be paying them out anyway."

"How many pies are left on my account?" asked Lundy. It seemed like a safe enough question, and one that would require no additional payment.

"Two meat and two fruit on yours; none on hers."

"Do you need pencils?" Lundy's smile was sweet as she swung her bookbag around and dipped her hand inside, pulling out three pencils. These ones were unsharpened, with perfect erasers. She had been carrying them for more than a year, since the dim, gnawing idea of going back had first occurred to her.

She had selected all her trade goods in threes, and she tried not to think about that, even as she knew, deep down, in the part of her that was still and would always be weeping, that Mockery had no more use for pencils or for pies. Mockery was over and done.

Vincent's eyes widened in earnest this time. He looked like he was fighting the urge to lick his lips as he said, "I always need pencils. They make keeping track of supplies much easier."

"These are better pencils than the last batch. They'd last you a long time, and the erasers haven't been used at all."

Vincent rallied, sensing a bargain in the making. "Yes, but I don't have a sharpener."

"Is that all?" Lundy smiled triumphantly as she produced a manual pencil sharpener from her pocket. "You could write everything down for a long, long time, if you had this."

This time, Vincent *did* lick his lips. "What do you want for it?"

It was a dangerous question. It was a trap. "What would be fair value? If ten meat pies and ten fruit pies each was fair value for two pencils that had already been used . . ."

"One of each, fruit and meat, every day, for a year."

"For all three—" Lundy caught herself. "For both of us?"

Vincent wrinkled his nose. "Yes," he said finally. "For both of you."

Lundy beamed as she put the pencils and sharpener down on the counter. Then she held out her hands. "Pies, please," she said.

They smelled like heaven. They smelled like coming home.

Lundy walked under the trees toward the Archivist's shack with her hands full of pies, meat and fruit and flaky crust begging her to sit down and eat them all up, to glut herself until her belly strained against the waistband of her skirt and everything made sense again. She refused to take even the smallest bite. Two of the pies were for Moon, and she knew if she tasted even a crumb, she wouldn't be able to stop herself. Friends didn't do that to friends.

It was funny. She had resigned herself to never having friends when she was so little that she barely remembered making the choice, and she didn't regret it, not for a moment. Most of the kids she went to school with couldn't see past her father to her, and the few who tried never seemed to like what they found when they reached her. She was too opinionated and too invested in following the rules. She liked the company of adults too much, she spent too much time reading. She was everything they didn't want to spend time with, and if it hadn't been for her father and for the reluctance many of them had to hit a girl, she would almost certainly have spent her weekends nursing black eyes and telling lies about where they'd come from.

Moon probably wasn't a very good friend. She was wild and she was strange and she followed the rules only because she knew she'd be punished if she didn't. She cared more about fair value than she did about anything else. And Lundy didn't care. Moon was her friend, her first friend and hence her best friend, and she was going to be so *happy* when she saw Lundy was back again. Back, with pies!

Maybe the pies would help Moon forgive her for running away when they were both hurt and grieving and confused. Death wasn't fair. Death wasn't fair value for *anything,* not for a world without Mockery, not for pies enough to touch the sky. But death didn't follow Market rules, and Lundy had been hurt and confused and worst of all, unsure, and feet had such a long memory. Her feet had remembered what it was to run home for comfort, and that was exactly what she'd done.

Lundy shivered with nerves as she stepped into

the clearing in front of the Archivist's hut, the trees heavy with their burden of birds. A few of the birds had disappeared in the two years she'd been gone, and new birds had replaced them. One, a snowy owl with eyes the color of the sky above a glacier, hooted mournfully at her.

"Who-who to you as well," she said politely. "You must not have been told to avoid asking questions. Who is Lundy, thank you and you're welcome, and who I'm looking for is Moon, and when I find her, we shall have pies." She felt terribly grown-up and pleased with herself, bringing paid-for pies to tell her friend that she was back again.

All that faded when the Archivist's door opened and the Archivist herself stepped onto the rickety porch. She stopped there, looking briefly startled before her expression softened, turning kind. "Lundy," she said. "I wasn't sure we'd be seeing you again."

"You still have books I need to read, ma'am," she said. "I brought pies for me, and for Moon." She stopped then, looking expectant. She didn't need to pay for Moon's location if she never asked for it, and waiting—especially silent waiting—could often work better than a question.

When she had first returned from the Goblin Market, she had sworn to herself and to her father (her father! Who would have thought that someone who had been to a place like this, had an

84

adventure like hers, could grow up to be as dull and ordinary as her *father?*) that she was never going to go back. The Market had hurt her, even if it had never intended to. It had *killed* Mockery. It hadn't given either of them fair value.

But she had known, hadn't she? Even then, she had known, because even then, she had been practicing her questions that weren't questions, finding ways to slide between the ask and the obligation. She had been intending to come back here from the moment that she'd left.

The Archivist nodded, slowly. "You were younger before," she said. "You still had a measure of protection about you, because no one wants to feel they've treated unfairly with someone who doesn't understand. You're not protected now."

"Yes, ma'am," said Lundy, who hadn't felt protected since she'd seen Mockery die.

"You *must* be careful, and you *must* follow the rules. You can't count on Moon to take your debts for you."

Lundy felt a pang of guilt. She had incurred two debts when she was in the Market for the first time, and Moon had taken them both, as per their agreement, without telling her exactly what that would mean. She assumed the other girl had paid them off by now.

Maybe she would have a debt Lundy could take, to keep things even between them.

"I will, ma'am."

The Archivist sighed again. "Oh, to be young, and innocent, and foolish." She pointed to a small trail into the woods. "She'll be by the stream this time of day. Remember, you didn't ask, but you indicated. What you find is yours to bear." She turned and went back inside.

Lundy frowned at the shack for a long moment before she walked toward the narrow trail. It was well worn, as if someone walked it regularly. She followed it, the smell of pie still in her nostrils, until she heard a stream chuckling to itself. She walked faster, coming around a small bend, and saw the familiar, hunched shape of Moon crouching on the bank.

"I came back!" she announced, pride and delight and joy in her tone.

Moon turned.

Lundy froze. It was the only thing she could think of to do; the only thing that wouldn't drop the pies.

The other girl's eyes were still wide and orange, but they had grown larger, seeming to swallow half her face, becoming fixed and staring in a way that human eyes had never been intended to be. Her lips were pursed and shiny and looked as hard as a beetle's shell—or a beak. And her fingers, oh. Her fingers had grown even longer, until they could no longer fold into fists.

"Hello, Lundy," said Moon.

"I came . . . I came back," repeated Lundy. "You . . ."

"Debts," said Moon. There was a smile in her voice, wry and sad, that never reached her pursed lips. "I was alone with you and Mockery gone, and I was sad and careless, and I guess I took too many. Now I'm almost tapped out, and the only fair value left for me will be the kind that flies away."

"You're . . ." Lundy stopped, swallowing hard. "You're becoming a bird."

"Yes." Moon blinked those impossible eyes. "I thought you knew. Do girls normally have orange eyes, in the world you're from?"

"No. But I don't know the world *you* came from. It could have been ordinary, for you." Lundy forced her legs to carry her closer. *It's not contagious,* she thought, and *all those cages,* she thought, and she had never wanted to run away more in all her life. "I brought pies."

"Did you give fair value?"

"Three pencils and a sharpener, and we both get pies for a year." She held out her left hand, offering its contents to Moon. "You must be hungry. Eat."

Moon started to reach out. Then she froze, and pulled her hands away. "I haven't paid for them."

"Two of the debts you carry are mine. Doesn't that mean I can give you pies to start paying them off? A *year* of pies, Moon. Isn't that worth anything?" They had both been there, when Mockery fell, when everything changed. Wasn't that worth anything?

"I . . ." Moon paused. "It might be." Carefully, she reached out and took a pie, closing her impossible eyes as she brought it to her hardened mouth.

Her first bite was more of a nibble than anything else, like she could no longer stretch her lips properly. Her second bite was more enthusiastic. By the end of the pie, she was gobbling, and she was smiling, her lips softening back into something ordinary, something *human*. She opened her eyes and beamed at Lundy.

"It was enough!" she crowed. "It was enough to give fair value! Thank you, thank you, *thank you!*"

Lundy held out the second pie, trying not to wonder what part of Moon's changed body represented her second debt. She had agreed, on that first dizzying visit, to take a debt for Moon, but she hadn't known what she was agreeing *to*. Shame came immediately on the heels of the thought. The debt was hers. If Moon wanted her to carry it, she could.

Besides, she thought. *Her eyes were orange before, but they weren't so big. Maybe every debt matters more when you're already carrying so many.*

As if she had read Lundy's thoughts, Moon

asked, shyly, "Do you want to take that debt for me now?"

No, thought Lundy, and, "Yes," said Lundy, and Moon slipped her hand into Lundy's. Her skin was cool, like it no longer regulated itself quite right. Like she needed a coat of feathers to protect her.

There was a tingling sensation that moved through Lundy's hands like a shiver. When Moon pulled away, her fingers were shorter, once more almost ordinary. Lundy looked at her own hand. Her nails were sharper, pointed like claws.

She looked up at Moon. Moon smiled at her hopefully.

"It's not so bad," she said. "You can pay that off, easy."

"Then let's get started," said Lundy.

7 FLY AWAY, FLY AWAY HOME

Moon was bird enough that she was perfectly comfortable sleeping in a tree, with only the night air to wrap around herself. Lundy, being still almost entirely a human girl, had other ideas about bedding. As the sun went down she found herself standing in front of the Archivist's shack, one hand raised in the beginning of a knock, unable to quite finish off the gesture.

She had sliced her own skin repeatedly with her sharp new nails, forgetting they were there when she went to brush her hair away from her face or scratch at a bug bite. If she slept outside where the mosquitos were, she would wake up flensed. But if the Archivist wanted fair value for sleeping on her floor . . .

The Goblin Market had seemed like a beautiful adventure on her first visit, a place where the rules made sense and the penalties were fair. Then it had become something terrible, a place where friends could die and not come back. Maybe the truth was somewhere in the middle of those two things, but now she understood how much there was to lose, and she was afraid.

Her hand was still raised to knock when the door opened and the Archivist looked at her. First at her face; then at her fingernails. A smile tugged at the corners of the Archivist's mouth.

"I see you found your friend," she said. "I assume you're looking for a place to sleep."

Afraid of questions she couldn't pay for, Lundy nodded silently.

"I have books that need to be organized. It will take some time. If you're willing to work an hour each night, I can give you a warm spot by the fire. Does that seem like fair value?"

An hour a night would leave plenty of time to go to the Market with Moon and look for ways to pay off her debt, to ease her closer to humanity. It might even leave time for Lundy to buy her own blunt fingernails back. She nodded enthusiastically. "That seems *wonderful*," she said.

"Excellent," said the Archivist, and beckoned her inside.

The books were in no particular order, and Lundy found the process of sorting them remarkably soothing, involving, as it did, a strange sort of scavenger hunt through the entire shack. Books had been used to prop up tables and level out shelves; they were piled on surfaces where books had no business being and tucked under the edge of the thin mattress of the Archivist's bed. In the case of books that had become load-bearing, Lundy used her school ruler to carefully note their heights and went searching for rocks or pieces of scrap wood that would do the job as well, if not better. In the case of books left too near to water or exposed to the air, she rolled her eyes and whisked them away to literary safety.

The books under the mattress gave her pause. She was standing there, trying to decide what should be done with them, when she heard a footstep behind her. Lundy turned. The Archivist looked at her kindly.

Lundy took strength from that expression, stood a little straighter, and asked, "What should I do with these?"

"Leave them. They have bad dreams, and I'm trying to help them tell themselves a little better."

After everything else she'd seen in the Goblin Market—centaurs who baked pies, children who turned into birds, fingernails that sharpened into talons—Lundy had no trouble with the idea of tucking books into bed to soothe them. "Oh," she said, and turned to go.

"No." The Archivist put a hand on her shoulder, stopping her. "Fair value means you're done for tonight, and should sleep. Children need their rest."

Lundy hesitated. "I've given fair value?"

"You have." The Archivist glanced at Lundy's clawed fingers. "Tomorrow, will you be looking for other ways to give fair value?"

"I left Moon alone when she was sad, and she got lost. I promised her I'd help her find the way back."

"Promises are their own form of fair value, as long as they're kept." The Archivist let go of Lundy's shoulder. "If you and Moon travel to the Market's edge, you'll find a man doing laundry by the stream. He's always looking for help, and few people offer it. Laundry is hard, sweaty work. But he pays well, because of its difficulty, and might be willing to clear a debt."

Lundy, who was used to debts being things owed to individuals, and not to entire communities, bit her lip and nodded. "May I ask a question?"

"You may, and if answering it would require payment, I will decline to answer."

"Why . . . why is Moon so deeply in debt, if it's that easy to clear debts away?"

"Come to the fire with me."

The Archivist turned and walked away, speaking as she went, so that Lundy had to follow or miss her words.

"You don't live here yet, if you ever will," said the Archivist. "You're a tourist, a summer person, coming through and moving on. That gives you a certain flexibility where the rules are concerned. People will be eager to find ways for you to clear any debts you acquire, because they don't want you carrying them with you into the wider world."

"Moon is the same age I am," said Lundy. "Why isn't she a summer person?"

"Moon was left here by her mother, who was once of ours, but who chose to leave us for a summer world, like yours," said the Archivist. "I don't know how she persuaded the door to open one last time. The door should not have opened. I have to believe she paid for it, somehow. But she left the child, and Moon took the oath of citizenship when she was barely higher than my knee. Perhaps she shouldn't have been allowed to do so. Perhaps she should have stayed a tourist, at least until she was old enough to see if the door to her mother's world would open for her. We were all she had. When she asked if we were going to send her away, what could we say but 'no' and 'never'? The rules make no exemptions for age. Once a citizen of the Goblin Market, always a citizen, and you'll pay as anyone else does. Everyone pays."

Lundy worried her lip between her teeth as she watched the Archivist lay out a pallet on the floor in front of the fire, creating a rough but serviceable bed. Finally, she asked, "What's the citizenship oath?"

"It is a promise you make to the Goblin Market, when you're sure you want to stay. A promise you make to yourself." The Archivist gave her a sidelong look. "Are you sure?"

Lundy—who had returned, despite the promise

she'd already made, because she was angry and hurt and sad and couldn't imagine spending one more minute among people who said one thing and meant another, who lied and cheated and looked down on her for not being gregarious, and soft, and kind, and all the things they believed a girl should be—shook her head, fast and fierce.

"No," she said. "I'm not sure. I didn't think . . . when I left before, I thought I was leaving for always. I didn't think I was coming back."

"Because you were sad."

"Because I was sad." Lundy looked at the Archivist with a child's innocent confusion, and asked, "Why did Mockery have to die?"

"All things die, child. It's part of giving fair value. Eventually, even the Market will die, and this world will become one more piece of the great graveyard that fills the walls between worlds. Your friend was very brave, and very clever, and she was cheated when she died too soon. But you and Moon were able to slay the Wasp Queen, even though she was older and wiser and more powerful than you were, weren't you?"

Lundy nodded silently, trying not to remember the way the brittle, terrible beast had screamed.

"That was the world trying to give fair value for something that shouldn't have happened so terribly soon. In the world you come from, unfair things can happen without consequences. Here, as soon as the Wasp Queen slew an innocent, she was doomed to lose."

"That doesn't seem fair either," said Lundy. "Mockery didn't do anything wrong."

"Sometimes 'fair' is bigger than just you," said the Archivist. She handed Lundy a pillow. "Sometimes 'fair' has to think about what's best for everyone. You don't have to be sure yet, Lundy. Remember the curfew. You still have time."

She turned and walked back to her own bed, lying down without undressing or brushing her teeth. That left Lundy unsure as to whether she should do those things, or whether the rules were different in the Goblin Market. She was older now. It seemed more important to have clean pajamas and a clean mouth before she went to sleep, like the Sandman—if he existed—might judge her for poor hygiene.

There was nothing to be done for it. She wasn't going to stay long. She had only come because she'd been angrier than her lingering sorrow over the loss of Mockery; she'd been intending to run away for a little while, to cool down and calm down and go back to school apologetic, after Mr. Holmen had had time to learn his lesson about treating girls like they were less than boys were. But Moon needed her here, and she couldn't run out on a friend, especially not a friend whose troubles were partially the result of Lundy's own mistakes.

And it wouldn't matter if Moon told her to go, anyway, because she couldn't leave at all, not while her fingernails were still claws, impossible things that had no place on a little girl's hands, that would mark her as a monster and worse outside the Goblin Market. Her father would weep if he saw them, would break down and cry as she had only seen him do once, the first time she'd returned. Her mother would never understand. Even Diana would shy away from her and scream. So no: she didn't have a choice.

Lundy stretched out on the blankets, her head resting on the pillow, which smelled like barley and lavender, and let the crackle of the fire soothe her into sleep.

When she woke, the shack was bright with sunlight streaming through the cracks in the walls. Lundy stretched luxuriously, trying not to grimace at the foul taste in her mouth. She *had* to find a way to brush her teeth if she was going to sleep here again. There was simply no way around it.

"Oh, good, you're up," said a voice.

Lundy screamed, sitting bolt upright and whipping around. Moon, who was crouched on the low table just inside the front door, blinked.

"You have some lungs on you," she said. "I bet you'd be a mockingbird. Or maybe one of those big parrots that can still talk no matter how big their beaks get. Not everybody gets to be a parrot. I always hoped I'd be one, until my first feathers came in brown." She plucked at one of the feathers tangled along her hairline.

Lundy's stomach sank as she realized that the feathers she'd naively assumed were some kind of fashion affectation were actually growing from Moon's scalp. No wonder Mockery had laughed when Lundy had asked her to braid a band of them into Lundy's own hair; no wonder her father had reacted so badly when she'd come home from the Goblin Market with them brushing against her shoulders. He must have thought that she'd already gone into debt.

Could girls even grow feathers in the world outside the Market? If she took Moon home with her—grabbed her right now and ran for the door—would the feathers fall out, or would they both be monsters for the rest of their lives, child-bird hybrids who belonged in a zoo more than they belonged in a classroom?

"Did I surprise you?" Moon sat back on her heels, looking apologetic. "I didn't mean to. But you've been asleep for so long, and I'm hungry, and the Archivist said we were going to go do some work today to try and pay off more of my debts."

"There's a man," said Lundy, finally getting her breath back. "He does laundry. She said he might let us help him."

"Oh." Moon's face fell. She held up hands which, while closer to normal than they had been, were still too long and thin to be anything other than changed. "I can't fold clothes very well. My fingers don't want to bend the right way."

"That's okay." One good thing about sleeping in her clothes: she was already dressed, and she felt like she could run a mile if she had to. "I'll do it. My hands are good, and once I pay back for the claws, they'll be even better. Then you can take the value and buy yourself off."

"I can't pay you for that kind of generosity."

"So we'll make another promise." Moon looked so small and lost that Lundy couldn't imagine *not* trying to help her. They had to help each other. If it wasn't a rule, it should have been: it should have been hanging in the hall with all the others. Lundy offered her a wan smile. "I'll do the work until you can help, and you can get more girl and less bird, and then if I need you to help me, you'll do it. That's fair value, right? The rules say it's okay for me to work for you if you're going to pay me sometime later. Like the rules said it was okay for you to do the bartering and get half of the pies."

"I think that's fair value," said Moon slowly. Then, more firmly, she said, "I *know* it's fair value. We've found fair value! Come on!"

She grabbed Lundy's wrist with her long, strange fingers, hauling her to her feet. Lundy didn't shudder from Moon's touch. Together, they ran out of the shack and down the path, skirting around the edge of the great breathing body of the Market until they came to a platform constructed to overhang the stream. There, a man so old and weathered that he could have been grandfather to them all was stirring great wooden tubs full of laundry with a stick.

He wrinkled his nose when he saw them coming, and said, "It's two buttons a load for something as soiled as what you're wearing, and I can't promise you'll have all the ribbons back when I'm finished."

"We're not here to ask you to do more work," said Lundy, who had always been good at being polite to adults, and could see that this wasn't a man who often had children seek him out for kindness. "We were hoping we could do some of the work for you. If you wouldn't mind."

The old man lifted his eyebrows, looking first at Lundy, and then at Moon's impossible fingers. "I'm too tired to be taking on debts for foolish little girls who couldn't mind fair value," he grumbled. "You'd have to accept the laundry yourself, not do what's already here, and you'd have to do it proper, no slacking off or lollygagging. It'll be hard and tiresome and not as fun as running wild in the woods all day."

"Yes, but at the end of it, we won't fly away," said Lundy. "I think we can tolerate a little hard work if it means we keep our feet on the ground."

Moon, who was closer to being a bird, and hence closer to the sky, looked unsure, but said nothing. She was still human enough to want to stay that way. The tipping point of her heart, if it existed, had not yet been reached.

The old man looked between them, and sighed. "All right," he said. "I could do with a rest. You can use my supplies, and in exchange you're to give me half of what you make. Soap doesn't grow on trees, you know, not unless the weather's gone strange." He went back to stirring his pot of laundry, which didn't feel much like resting to Lundy, but what did she know? She wasn't an old man, and she didn't operate her own business. She couldn't call it "owning," because there was no building, or sign, or business card—all the things she had learned to associate with the idea of owning a thing.

She and Moon sat on some rocks off to the side, and waited for people to bring their washing.

The first to arrive was a beleaguered-looking man with a long cow's tail and four children trotting along behind him. All of them had tails like his, and the two girls had curving horns growing from their foreheads, on which they had tied a remarkable number of bows. His arms were full of clothes, which he tried to thrust at the old man.

"Not me, not today," the old man said, and

hooked a finger at Lundy and Moon. "These clever young things are working off a spot of debt. Give what wants doing to them. Payment's as standard, and their work will be up to snuff or I'll take fair value out of their hides."

The cow-man—or bull-man, Lundy supposed— looked dubious, but handed his washing over anyway. "It all needs to be clean by high-sun," he said. "The children will have found a mud puddle or something of the like by then, and we'll have to start all over again."

"You can count on us, sir," said Lundy brightly. "It'll be clean as anything."

The bull-man still looked dubious. But one of the children had found a frog and was on the verge of pursuing it into the stream, and two more of them were already halfway up a tree, and the fourth was poking a stick into a hole, and it was clear he didn't have the time to argue about laundry.

"Fine," he said. "But I won't pay until I'm back, and I won't pay for anything I don't receive."

"Fair value," agreed Lundy, and smiled prettily as the bull-man rounded up his children and ushered them away, to potentially less muddy climes.

When she turned, the old man was looking at her. "Well?" he said. "Get washing."

Doing laundry by hand was even harder and less pleasant than Lundy, who had grown up with a washing machine, could ever have imagined. First they had to wet the clothes all the way down, and it seemed like the fabric fought this process, refusing to soak through even though she knew, just *knew* that everything would have been drenched in an instant if she hadn't wanted it to be. Then they had to beat the wet clothes against some rocks the old man had placed for that purpose, breaking up the stains, and *then* came the soap, and the scrubbing, and the wringing-out.

Lundy had never cared for doing laundry. After an afternoon spent by the stream, washing other people's clothing by hand, she thought she would welcome the chance to do it every day, forever, as long as she got to use the machine. The machine was *heaven*.

But the bull-man came back for his clothes, and was quietly pleased to find them clean and dry and ready, and he paid the man who owned the soap and barrels a handful of glittering sand, and some of the feathers fell out of Moon's hair.

But the woman with the snails slithering through her hair came back for her flowing gowns, and was surprised and delighted to find them clean and damp and ready, and she paid the man a handful of empty snail shells that clattered like bones, and somehow the lines of Moon's face relaxed so that her orange eyes were only human-sized, and not large and round as buttons.

Over and over, their customers came back for their things and found fair value had been more than given, and they paid, how they paid! The old man looked more and more satisfied as their day's take increased, until he turned to them as the sun was setting and said, "You have done better than I had any right to expect you to. Come back anytime."

He handed Lundy a silver coin with tarnish along the edge, like a small and captive moon, and the talons fell from her fingers, leaving them stubby and childlike once again. She felt an unexpected pang of regret, like she had just given up something precious, which made no sense at all. How could having claws possibly be precious?

Moon, whose eyes were still orange, who still had feathers in her hair, but who otherwise looked like an ordinary child, beamed at her. "Look how much we did in a day!" she crowed. "You're my lucky charm."

Lundy, who had some questions about how Moon had been able to amass so much debt if she could pay it all off in a single day's work, tucked the coin away in her pocket and smiled. "I guess somebody has to be," she said. "Let's go home."

And so they did.

8 BY THE FIRE

Moon lay in a heap next to the Archivist's fire, snoring with openmouthed gusto. The Archivist looked at her, amused, before returning her attention to Lundy.

"You want to know about debt," she said.

Lundy, who had raised no such questions, blinked. Then she nodded. "Yes. I do."

"I told you it would be easier for you because you don't belong here yet. As long as you're a tourist, people will pay you generously. Your enjoyment is a part of fair value, until you make your mind up one way or the other."

Lundy, who had not enjoyed the fight against the Wasp Queen or the death of her friend, frowned. "Moon was so close to becoming a bird. Her hands, and her eyes, and—I don't understand how people can do that to each other."

"We don't do it to each other, child. Can you not see that? We take so much care *not* to do that to each other that it's a wonder we don't all walk around with ledgers in our hands, measuring our breaths to be sure we've contributed enough to the world we live in to justify them. We make our bargains based upon an innate sense of fairness, and the Market listens when we say we've received the value we require. Because this is the Market at work, make no mistake of that. I told you when you were younger that we began with a single peddler's son. Do you remember?"

Lundy nodded silently.

"He was lost and lonely and trying to survive, and the world saw something in him. The doors began to open more often, bringing him companions. The Market grew up around him as more people came, and stopped, and stayed. But there was no single currency everyone could agree upon, and hoarding any given sort of money was a gamble—maybe a door would open to a world where that kind of coin could spend and maybe it wouldn't. Barter became the order of the day. The trouble is, barter opens questions of relative value. Do you understand?"

This time, Lundy shook her head.

"Consider your pies. You enjoy having a full belly, and you must like the taste of them, since you returned to the same food stall when it was time to make a new bargain. To you, the pies were worth whatever you paid for them. To the piemaker, whatever you offered was worth more than the pies. Now, imagine for a moment that you were so hungry you feared you might die. What would have stopped the piemaker from taking everything you had in exchange for a handful of crumbs?"

"I wouldn't have let him," said Lundy firmly.

"But again, imagine you were *ravenous,* you were starving, that hunger had wrapped its hands so tightly around your bones that you couldn't think straight. There is wanting and there is needing, and when you want, you can make good choices, but when you *need,* it's important the people around you not be looking to take advantage. When there are no clear prices, only the nebulous idea of 'fair value,' people get hurt. People get cheated. We had some bad bargains in the beginning, when folks looked at what we were building here and saw themselves as rich and powerful, while the rest of us existed only to fill their pockets with everything we had."

Lundy, who had met her share of bullies, said nothing.

"One day, all those people who had started bargaining in bad faith, who had looked to take advantage or not fulfilled their agreements to the best of their abilities, woke up and found they wore the signs of their failures on their faces. They had feathers in their hair. They had beaks, or talons, or stranger. And the ones who realized they'd been negligent with their fellows, who worked to make things right, found themselves back the way they had been in fairly short order. The ones who didn't . . ." The Archivist looked meaningfully toward the door, and through it toward the clearing where the birdcages hung.

Lundy's dinner—chicken pie in flaky pastry—seemed suddenly sour in her stomach. "What happened to them?"

"Most flew away. Some had done things so terrible that they were locked up for the protection of those around them. A few stayed free, and worked their way back toward their original shapes. Most who become birds now follow their example. It takes a very long time. There's not much a bird can do to provide fair value." Seeming to catch the direction of Lundy's thoughts, the Archivist smiled. "The chickens we raise are only that: chickens. You haven't eaten the vicar."

"What's a vicar?" asked Lundy, and sagged in relief.

The Archivist ignored her question, which may have been for the best. "Most of the children who live at the Market spend at least some time as a bird. It teaches them to be frugal in their bargains and mindful of their obligations. Their parents are happy to help them find value that can be done on two good wings, unless they've become some sort of flightless bird, and then we find other ways. Moon doesn't have a parent to step in for her. Had she made it all the way into her cloak of feathers, I would have been forced to stir myself to find her things an owl could do to buy the way back to girlhood. It's only a permanent condition if the one transformed allows it to be, continuing to be indolent or greedy until their mind fades into the mind of a bird."

Lundy frowned deeply. "My grandpa was sick for a long time before he died," she said. "What happens if someone's too sick to give fair value?"

"Health is a thing that can be bought, as can everything worth bartering," said the Archivist. "But if someone truly cannot give fair value— if they are undergoing childbirth, for example, or if the health they need must be purchased by someone else, because they were injured or sickened too quickly to make their own bargain— the world is forgiving. This is the Market acting, to balance itself, to keep us happy and hale and working together, not draining one another dry in the name of personal enrichment. A new parent, weary from bringing a life into the world, may be waited upon hand and foot for weeks, their every need met, their every desire catered to, and still be seen as owed something, for the great good they have done us. How do you balance out the fair value of a life? And it's true that sometimes, one who has lived long enough to feel themselves finished will allow their health to decline, so they might slip away quietly. The ones who choose to care for such individuals will also find their needs met, without any exchange other than their compassion. The Market *knows,* you see, when someone is acting to the best of their ability. The Market doesn't punish us for having limitations.

It only reminds us that fair value applies to everyone."

"Oh." Lundy sat quietly for a time, considering all these things, before she stood. "So I should do my sorting for the night, before I go to sleep."

The Archivist smiled. "Yes," she said. "You should."

Lundy woke once again to sunlight streaming through the cracks in the walls, but more, to a feeling of deep contentment that began at the soles of her feet and spread all the way through her body, filling her. She stretched and the contentment stretched with her, purring like a cat, reassuring her that everything that could possibly be well was well, and would remain so.

Moon was still asleep, curled into a tight ball. Some of the feathers had fallen out of her hair in the night. Lundy picked up one of them, turning it over in her hand before tucking it behind her ear. It tickled. She left it there, standing and stretching again, this time with her feet flush to the ground. The motion brought a whiff of sour skin-smell up to tickle her nose. She grimaced. Her clothes were mostly clean, thanks to spending a whole day doing laundry and soaking herself in soapy water, but the soap had never quite reached most of her skin. She needed a bath in the very worst of ways.

The last time she'd been here, she had been

eight years old and perfectly content to bathe in the chilly stream, laughing and splashing at Moon as they scrubbed themselves clean. Later, Mockery had joined them, older and wilder and bringing a measure of obedience in her wake. Now, though . . . even at ten, her body was beginning to do things she wasn't sure she appreciated, widening in places and narrowing in others, while her chest ached at odd hours and in ways that she didn't have the proper words for. Her mother said she was growing up. Lundy was fairly sure there was no bargain in the world that could give her fair value for *that*.

So no, she didn't want to bathe in the stream, naked and exposed to anyone who came along. But she remembered seeing a bathhouse on the far side of the Market, with tubs of hot water and soap for the asking. It seemed like something worth exploring further. She considered Moon for a moment before nudging the other girl with her toe.

"I want a bath," she said. "Wake up."

Moon grumbled.

"I want a bath, and you *need* a bath. Do birds not bathe? You smell like a henhouse. Wake up."

Moon rolled over and cracked open one owl-orange eye. Lundy found herself obscurely glad that even though Moon's fingers were now of an ordinary length, and Moon's eyes were now of an ordinary size, they were still orange. She wasn't sure she would have been able to see her friend looking out of any other color.

"You're mean," Moon said. "I'm not a chicken."

"That doesn't mean you can't *smell* like one," said Lundy primly. "Come on. Let's go get baths."

"Don't wanna pay for a bath."

It was becoming clearer how Moon was able to keep getting herself into debt. If she didn't seek out baths on her own, someone would eventually chuck her into a lake to stop the smell, and then there was every chance the Market would punish her for not giving fair value to the noses around her. Lundy rolled her eyes. "I have my whole schoolbag still, and it's *full* of things," she said. "I can buy you a bath. But then you have to do something to get me back. I don't care what. We have to give fair value to each other."

"I'll show you where the best berry bushes are," said Moon, climbing to her feet, suddenly interested now that the bill would be going to someone else. "They weren't blooming last time you came, but they're so good now, we can even pick and bring them back and sell them for something to drink with our dinner."

"It's a deal," said Lundy. She beamed at Moon, and Moon beamed back, and she couldn't remember why she had ever thought leaving this wonderful place was a good idea. She'd been sad, yes, but she'd been sad at home, too, and no one there had understood why. Here, at least, she was among people who could *see* her. Who might listen.

They left the Archivist's shack and took each other's hand, running side by side down the path that ringed the Market, Lundy's schoolbag banging against her hip with every step, Moon pulling her onward. Lundy allowed herself to be led, paying attention to everything around her for the day when she would be making her own way.

In a distant way, she realized she was making plans for the future. A future *here,* in the Goblin Market. Maybe that would change. Maybe she would remember the husband she had always assumed would one day come along, would remember the library she had imagined herself organizing, would find something to love and live for in the world where she'd been born . . . but more and more, none of those things felt likely.

"I have to go home soon," she said, and her words were hollow, obligations spoken where the wind could hear them, and not things that lingered in the chambers of her heart.

"Soon isn't now," said Moon, and hauled her onward, onward, ever onward.

Two buttons and a spool of thread bought them all the hot water and soap and privacy they could want. Moon stripped without shame once they were in their shared room, letting Lundy—who was still a little shy about the idea of being naked in front of someone else—do the same. Feathers grew out of Moon's shoulder blades, a long row of white and gold that pressed close down against the skin but fluffed out when she settled down into the water of her tub.

"Ah," said Moon, sinking deeper and closing her eyes. "That's good. You're smart, Lundy. You have good ideas."

"Thank you," said Lundy primly, and stepped into her own tub. The water was so hot it stung her skin, leaving it tingling. She sank slowly onto her butt, letting her legs float up until her ankles were almost level with her knees. What would it be like, to have feathers, to get them wet? Did Moon feel trapped by the knowledge that she couldn't fly away, or did she feel free because she was more human than she'd been? "Can I ask you something?"

"You paid for the baths," said Moon. "You can ask me anything."

It was a grand offer, one that made the air feel as tingly as the water. Lundy shifted a little, uncomfortable. How was it that Moon could *live* here, could feel the power of a Market debt tugging and transforming her skin, but not understand how big an answer that was? It didn't seem right.

"Do you ever wish you hadn't chosen the Market?"

114

Moon opened one eye, looking thoughtfully at Lundy. "You mean because of the feathers?"

"Yes." The feathers, and other things. She thought of Moon's bleak eyes, of her saying that the only fair value left would be the kind that flew away. "You were . . . you were so sad, and you looked so strange, like you were forgetting who you were."

"It was the fingers." Moon held her ordinary hands up for Lundy to see. "I've been pretty tapped out before, but I was always young enough that the Market left me with hands. I think it doesn't want to make birds out of the really *little* kids, because they might forget to be human and just fly away. These days, there's enough for me to care about that I don't want to fly off and be an owl forever. That happens sometimes, with people who go too deep into debt. The Market dresses them in feathers, and they forget they were ever anything else, and they can be happy. It only happens to *little* kids if they're so sad being people that being birds is better. The rest of us get feathers in our hair, and maybe mouths that don't move right, and we try harder, because it's not fun to have a beak when you don't want to. This was the first time I was old enough for the Market to start taking away my hands."

She pulled them back into the water with the rest of her, sighing.

"You were gone, and Mo . . . Mockery was

gone, and I wanted to pretend I was special, I guess," she said, stumbling over their lost friend's name. "That I was the one the Market loved so much that it would let me bend the rules more than it let anyone else. The one it would take care of and protect. It was silly of me? But I don't have any parents to tuck me in or tell me to brush my hair, and I wanted to believe the Market loved me. The Market does love me. It loves us all. It just . . . loves the rules more. It doesn't let any of us break them. It punishes us when it has to, because the rules have to be for everyone if they're going to be for anyone."

"Even for kids," said Lundy.

"Even for kids and tourists," said Moon. "I'll work off the rest of my debt, and then we can practice not going into debt together, you and me. Soon isn't now. Soon doesn't have to be ever. You're going to stay this time, right? I feel like we'd be best friends, if you stayed."

"I'm going to stay," said Lundy, and she was lying, and neither of them knew it then, but both of them would know it soon enough.

9 WITH RIBBONS FOR HER HAIR

The Lundy who had stepped through the door for her second visit to the Goblin Market would barely have recognized the one who came stumbling through it for her second return to the world of her birth. *This* Lundy was thin, her arms and legs wiry with new muscle, rendered lean by physical labor and the rigors of questing. *This* Lundy had bruises on her ribs and a narrow scar down the middle of her back, tracing the outline of her spine, where the Bone Wraiths had tried to set their captive countryman free of the fetters of her flesh.

This Lundy was dressed in patchwork and tatters, with her hair cut short in a pageboy bob and thin leather straps wrapped around her fingers to protect them. But most of all—oh, most of all—*this* Lundy had feathers in her hair, short bronze feathers that glimmered when the light hit them. They grew at the nape of her neck, exposed by the shortness of her haircut, and it would have been possible for the casual observer to tell themselves she had merely tied them there, the fashion stylings of a child.

She had earned each of them with a debt as yet unpaid to the Goblin Market, and she had done so intentionally. They were a mark of promises as yet unkept, and they were, in their own way, a promise entirely on their own. She would return. She would go back to the Market with fuller pockets and a firmer plan, and perhaps this time, she would stay forever, as she had promised a girl with owl-orange eyes that she would one day do. With feathers in her hair she walked through the darkened school to the doors, and out into the evening. She looked at the empty parking lot with quest-wearied eyes. How small the world she'd come from looked now! How narrow and gray!

Home always shrinks in times of absence, always bleeds away some of its majesty, because what is home, after all, apart from the place one returns to when the adventure is over? Home is an end to glory, a stopping point when the tale is done. Lundy walked across the parking lot with the smooth, easy stride of a predator, and no one came to challenge her or ask her where she'd been.

She walked down the moonlit streets of her home town, and everything was peaceful, and everything was still. Somewhere in the distance an owl cried. If she went after it, found it perched in some high tree or in the eaves of some old house, it would look at her with avian incomprehension, incapable of seeing her as a human being, as a friend. A bird in this world was only a bird.

Lundy walked on.

On an ordinary street sat an ordinary house, the windows dark, the occupants still. Lundy plucked the spare key from behind a loose brick in the decorative flowerbed and let herself in, closing the door silently in her wake. In the morning, there would be screams of joy and shouts of accusation. In the morning, her father would see the feathers in her hair and weep. Here, however, now, there was only the night, and her own bed, too soft and too big, like a cotton-wrapped cloud, and she had come a very long way. She was very tired. She had only intended to stop long enough to fill her pockets, but she was so tired, and surely a brief nap couldn't hurt?

Lundy slept. The tale continued.

PART III
WHERE WE WOULD BE

10 IN WHICH A QUEST BEGINS AND ENDS

The Chesholm School for Girls was considered a jewel in the crown of private education: expensive, exclusive, and capable of taking the most misguided of young women and turning them into the most proper of young ladies. Tuition was steep, of course, but every penny was justified by the rigorous nature of the curriculum and isolated location of the campus. There would be no shenanigans here, not under the watchful eye of the professionally trained staff.

(When Lundy had been informed she'd be going away to boarding school "for her own good," she hadn't been surprised. She had, after all, disappeared twice to the sort of place that was only meant to exist in children's books and fairy stories—a place that remembered her father by face, even if it never spoke his name. He had chosen to put the Goblin Market behind him as soon as he possibly could, and he wanted the same for her. The fear and yes, longing in his eyes when he looked at the feathers growing from the nape of her neck had only confirmed her calm, quiet belief that there had never been any other choice available to him.)

("The doors only find you when you're alone, and since I can't keep you safe here, I'm sending you someplace where you'll never be alone," he'd said, and that had been enough for him, even as it could never have been enough for her, even as it could never have been the answer.)

Here at the Chesholm School, the student body wore uniforms designed to prevent feelings of inequality, masking all physical failings and advantages under layers of thick, shapeless cotton and regulation-length skirts. Some of the older girls had been sent away by their parents for harboring "unnatural urges"—one of many subjects the teachers refused to discuss in any detail with the younger girls, who were left to wonder whether their adored upperclassmen were secretly jewel thieves or necromancers—and had a tendency to disappear, hand in hand, around the edges of empty classrooms. Most of the younger girls had been sent away for truancy, or lying, or parental disobedience.

Most: not all. Lundy was far from the only runaway, although a few days of careful inquiry had confirmed that she was the only one who'd run off somewhere that technically shouldn't have existed. The others had run off to exciting, faraway places with names like "Cleveland" and "Bar Harbor," chasing their dreams in the form of Greyhound buses and distant relatives who'd

promised that a smart, savvy girl who didn't mind getting her hands dirty could work on their ocelot farms, or in their herb gardens, or in their nurseries.

Some girls fought the Chesholm methods, cutting up their uniforms with sewing scissors, going on health strikes against the perfectly nutritionally balanced, totally flavorless meals. Others sank into the school with what Lundy could only view as a full-body sigh of relief, the bruises on their wrists fading, the wariness in their eyes retreating, if never entirely going away.

During her first term there, one of the girls had been removed from their shared dormitory when her belly, despite the careful portions and general lack of second helpings, had begun to swell all out of proportion to her slender frame. That girl had been gone for most of a semester, and when she had returned, she had been quiet, and whittled-down in a way Lundy didn't have a name for, only the quiet, cruel awareness of its reality.

She had slipped that girl her own desserts for the rest of the year, until summer break had come calling and cleared them all off-campus for a brief return to home and supposed normalcy. When the girl—whose name was something mild and ordinary, and which Lundy had never quite been able to trap on her tongue, having taken to regarding the use of other people's proper names as uncouth—had asked her why, it had taken Lundy some time to find the words. Finally, in a faintly baffled tone, she had said, "The school took something away from you, and they aren't giving you fair value. I just didn't want you to think that no one cared about the debts."

That girl hadn't returned to school at the end of break. Sometimes Lundy wondered about her, with her huge, sad eyes and her hollowed-out middle, not yet seventeen and already broken by people who thought children couldn't be owed debts when things were done to them, when things were stolen. She wondered if there was a door somewhere, maybe labeled with an entreaty to be sure, that the girl could walk through and find herself finally safe, finally home.

She hoped so.

Lundy herself fit in reasonably well, once she understood what "fitting in" meant. Her love of rules was still intact, and while the school rules weren't hung on the walls at regular intervals, they were printed in the student handbook, and they were discussed at mandatory assemblies. Girls were required to grow their hair to a certain length, which came with the convenient side effect of hiding the feathers: her father had plucked them one by one on the morning when he'd woken to find her curled in her bed, and every one of them had hurt, every one of them had bled, and every one of them had grown back.

They represented a debt as yet unpaid to the Goblin Market; they wouldn't go away so easily.

It had been easy to return after her first trip, when she had been eight years old and easily forgiven for getting lost. The word "runaway" had never crossed anyone's mind, at least so far as Lundy was aware. The truth had been a secret uneasily kept between her and her father, and it had burned, cast adrift in a space where there had never previously been any need for secrets. What should have brought them closer had instead pushed them incrementally further apart, unable to find the commonalities that had led them both to an impossible door, led them both through to the wonders on the other side.

Returning from her second trip had been . . . harder. Everyone in her classroom had seen her fight with Mr. Holmen, had seen the way she looked at him, had heard her declare her intent to walk away. They had just never expected her to walk so *far*. Most of them had no idea how far she'd gone. Only her father had known, looking at the feathers growing soft and downy at the nape of her neck; only her father had *understood*.

Only her father had had the authority to enroll her at the Chesholm School, with its narrow, uncomfortable beds, and its narrow, uncomfortable halls, and the narrow, uncomfortable eyes of authority staring at her from every nook and cranny. He had seen the leaving in her eyes, the desire to charge right back into her impossible adventure—had seen that somehow, his world, his *real* world, had become the way station, while the Goblin Market was fast becoming home—and he had done his best to keep her put by sending her away.

It seemed like a terribly backward way of doing things, but what did she know? She was, as the world seemed to delight in reminding her, a child: ten years old when she had run away to the Goblin Market, and still ten years old when she had returned with no intention of staying.

Eleven came to call while she was locked in orientation at the Chesholm School, bringing with it not lemon cake and streamers, but a lecture from the headmistress on the responsibility of young ladies to keep themselves above reproach, unsullied and untouchable by the world around them. Lundy listened politely, trying to hear the fair value in her words, which sounded like the screeching of so many birds, and when they were done she removed herself to her room, which she shared with three other girls—including the one with the sad eyes, whose belly had yet to begin to swell—and wept.

Twelve followed a year later, falling predictably in line with all the birthdays that had come before it. The changes Lundy had been noticing in her body accelerated, aching hips spreading and breasts budding, until her family had to send money for a new set of uniforms, until the unasked-for indignity of change culminated in waking in a pool of her own blood, the feathers on her neck itching wildly. They, too, had grown in the night, and when she touched them, her baby feathers fell away in her hand, leaving adult plumage in their wake.

She smuggled those fallen feathers to the library, where an afternoon's research informed her that, were her debts to become too great, she would take to the air as a raptor of some kind, most likely a golden eagle, proud and wild and not subject to such mammalian cruelties. That night she dreamt of flying, soaring high and free above the land, and nothing could catch her, or touch her, or bring her back to earth. She dreamt of Moon and Mockery, standing beneath her, watching how she caught the wind.

That night, Lundy began plotting her escape.

It was not difficult to begin modifying the pattern of her days. The habit of friendship had never come easily to her, and while most of the other students thought reasonably well of her, when they thought of her at all, none of them counted her as a close companion. It was a small thing to withdraw, to choose the library over the gaming field, the empty classroom over the cafeteria. The staff at the Chesholm School were meant to ensure that every student had proper exercise and access to fresh air, but the reality of things was that the quiet girls, the patient girls, the girls who didn't make waves or make trouble, could effectively do as they liked when not in class.

Lundy did her lessons, did her chores, and watched the doors, waiting for one of them to shift in its frame, to become something it wasn't intended to be. Weeks went by with no such transformation. She began to question whether it was ever going to happen at all.

This, she finally realized, was the true intent of her banishment; she was meant to begin questioning what had happened to her, where she had gone, what she had seen. She was meant to forget Moon and Mockery, and the Archivist, and the taste of Vincent's pies. And maybe she could have done it, maybe she could have left them behind, if not for the patch of impossible feathers on the nape of her neck. Children did not sprout feathers in this world. If she had sprouted feathers, she must have done it somewhere else. The only other world she could remember was the Goblin Market—which meant the Market was real, and this slow, grinding extinction of the child she had been was nothing more than an attempt to keep her away from it.

She was staring at a closet door when she caught a flicker of motion and turned to see one of her classmates walking down the hall, a stack of books tucked under her arm. Lundy frowned.

"Hello," she said. The other girl looked up, apparently startled to hear herself addressed. "Do you come this way often?"

"Every day," said the girl, with a look on her face that clearly indicated she was questioning Lundy's sanity. She hurried onward, not offering any further conversation.

Still frowning, Lundy gave the closet another thoughtful look. The first door had been in a tree, and there had been no one else around. The second door had been in the school hallway, yes, but the hall had been empty, hadn't it? The middle of the day meant people were locked in their classrooms, by and large, and there had been no one there to see her go.

That was the reason her father had selected a school guaranteed to turn a rebellious child into an obedient one, promising an absolute absence of privacy. She couldn't remember the last time she'd been entirely unsupervised. She was never alone, and the doors couldn't find her.

That needed to change.

Lundy looked over the school activities the next day, considering each of them in turn until she found one which seemed to fit her needs. Neatly, she put her name down on the list. The upperclassman who was meant to be supervising the signups looked at her quizzically.

"Birdwatching?" she asked. "Really? You've never struck me as the naturalist type."

Having gone out of her way not to strike anyone as any type of anything, Lundy smiled politely. "I appreciate birds," she said. "And my father's latest letter said if he felt I was making more of an effort to participate in the life of the school, he might let me come home at the end of the term. I want to show that I'm willing."

The upperclassman smirked, as if to say that no one ever *really* left the Chesholm School behind. But she stamped Lundy's application for the birdwatching club all the same, and handed her a notebook with an attached pencil, so she could start writing down the birds she saw.

Birds I want to see, thought Lundy, dutifully recording sparrows and blackbirds and crows. *Owl. Eagle. Moon. Me.*

She started slow, following the assigned trails, writing down the common birds that were too slow or too stupid to avoid the school. She showed her lists to their faculty advisor every other Tuesday, when the club held its official meetings. She sat at the back of the room and made notes, which she willingly shared with anyone who asked. She thought this was fair value for the freedom to rove farther and farther from the school building itself, following the promise of rare bird sightings away from the thick stone walls that held no future for her.

Every time she went out, she carried a handful of potential trade goods with her, hiding them in the hollow of an old hickory tree. By the end of six weeks, she felt rich from all the pencils and buttons and bright-colored ribbons she had hidden there, enough to pay for food and lodging for an entire season at the Market.

Only once did another student catch her in the act of accessing her cache, another upper-classman, this one an exile for "unnatural urges," a phrase Lundy still didn't quite understand. The teen stared at her across the clearing. Lundy froze with her hand inside the hickory, barely daring to breathe.

"They won't announce it, but Miss Henley who does the Thursday night patrol has the flu and no one wants to take her shift, so there's not going to be a Thursday night patrol," said the older girl, voice low, in case someone might come along and overhear her. "If you're going to run, you should do it then, when there's nobody looking."

The teen walked away, leaving Lundy's head spinning. This could be a trap. It didn't feel like a trap, but the good traps never did, did they? If every trap felt like a trap, they'd never catch anyone.

But the woods at night, with a full bag and no one to stop her . . . it was a temptation too great to be denied. Lundy swallowed her fear and her concern and returned to the classroom, sitting with her hands folded in her uniformed lap, listening as the teacher droned on about comportment and manners and the importance of not bringing shame to the family, and her thoughts were full of beating wings and the sweet smell of impossible fruits.

Later—when her parents were summoned to the school in the wake of her disappearance, when her father and the headmaster were flinging accusations back and forth like a golden ball— her teachers would say she'd been attentive and polite during her last days with them, that she had listened more closely than ever before, participating in class discussions with the passion of the converted. "We felt like we were finally reaching her," they would say, and their words would be defensive apology and lament at the same time, because the teachers of the Chesholm School truly *believed* in the work they were doing, truly *believed* they could, with hard work and strict discipline, lead the children in their care to a better life.

Later, the school would say she'd run away, and her father would point to the literature where they bragged about their unclimbable fence, their professional security teams, and ask how that was possible. He would say she must have been taken, telling a little lie to cover the huge, inconvenient truth that she had run so far that she might never be recovered, so far that she had crossed into another, impossible world rather than spend one more minute in this one. The authorities would become involved. Money would change hands—what the school would consider blood money, paid for silence, and Franklin Lundy would consider fair value for a daughter, and silently, secretly bill against the Goblin Market in his dreams.

But that is all later.

When Thursday arrived, creeping into the present one day at a time, as days are wont to do, Lundy rose, dressed, and went about her day as she always did. No one noticed her slipping an extra apple into her pocket at lunch, or taking a handful of pencils from the supply cupboard in her English class. She might not have become a better student during her time at the Chesholm School, but she had definitely become a better thief. She counted off the minutes of her classes with her hands folded on her desk and her eyes on the teachers, giving no outward sign that anything was wrong. She needed, more than anything, to be seen as normal.

The feathers on the back of her neck itched, edges brushing against her skin until it was almost maddening, and she didn't scratch, and she didn't draw attention to herself. She was going back where they could be paid off, where fair value could be achieved—or its opposite, where she could allow herself to slide peacefully into debt and feel the sky stretched out around her in a loving embrace, talons spread and wings bearing her ever on. She was going *home*.

The final bell rang. She rose with the others, and returned to her dorm to collect her bird-watching things. Her active and enthusiastic club participation was well known within her dorm. No one questioned her planning an after-dinner excursion. She had filed all the appropriate forms, gathered all the appropriate permissions.

No one questioned anything, until she walked into the woods and did not come back.

Lundy walked through the trees with a spring in her step and the weight of her bag hanging against her hip, every pilfered pencil and stolen scrap of ribbon reassuring her that she was going, she was on her way. There was no turning back now. Evening walks were allowed for birdwatchers, but they were logged out and logged back in, and by now the upperclassman in charge of watching the register would surely have noticed that she was running late.

She'd been walking for more than an hour, heading deeper and deeper into the trees surrounding the campus. Strange sounds called to her from out of the foliage, the cries of owls and the rustling of nocturnal animals. She ignored them. Nothing here could frighten her, not after the things she'd seen and done and faced in the Goblin Market. What did a few noises have on the Bone Wraiths, on the Wasp Queen? This was a test at most, a distraction at least, and so she walked on.

Her feet hurt. Her legs, no longer accustomed to traveling miles in a single session, ached, and her thighs chafed where they rubbed together. If not for the feathers on the back of her neck, she might have started to believe what her father had said before committing her to boarding school— that she had had a dream, wonderful and terrible and untrue, and now was the time to wake up. She might have turned back.

But the feathers on the back of her neck were real. It hurt when she tugged on them, and as her mammalian body had undergone puberty, they, too, had changed, growing longer and stronger and darker. Even for a bird, she was no longer a fledgling. And if she wasn't a fledgling, she could walk.

She walked until she saw a tree that looked like it belonged to a different forest, twisted until there wasn't a straight line anywhere in its trunk or in its branches, with leaves in a dozen delicate shades of green. Lundy's breath caught. She did not hurry, but angled toward it as a flower angles toward the sun.

When she drew closer, she saw that at the center of its trunk, there was a door, and that graven on the door were two simple words:

BE SURE.

"I am," she whispered, and pushed the door open, and stepped through, and was gone.

11 IN AIR AS CLEAR AS CRYSTAL

Lundy stepped out of the impossible hall and into the comforting, golden-lit darkness of the Market by night. Candles, paper lanterns, and colorful glass lamps hung from wagons and stalls, providing enough illumination to see by, if not to do fine needlework or read. She didn't need to do either of those things. As if in a dream, she wandered toward the first rank of sellers.

A few were still open, despite the lateness of the hour. They looked at her uniform, at her legs, long and gawky with the latest attack of puberty upon her frame, and politely looked away. The clothing booths were closed for the night, and she was dressed; there was no value to be had in pulling a seamstress or tailor from their bed and thrusting her at them.

Surprisingly few of them recognized her, for she was a child no longer: her hair, which had never been very long before, or terribly well tended, hung loose down her back, secured with a ribbon tied *just so,* according to the exacting standards of the Chesholm School. Her skin, which had been dirty and bruised and freckled in the way of Market children, was clean. Even her uniform, too short and too tight in the chest, marked her as a teenager. It was rare for someone to begin visiting at such a late age. It was not unheard of. And so Lundy walked past the homes and businesses of people who had once brought her their laundry, or clucked their tongues when she tumbled into mud puddles in front of them, and not one of them stopped her, or said a word in greeting.

Her progress was neither smooth nor steady. She tripped over the uneven ground, her heavy school shoes uniquely unsuited to the terrain. She stopped, over and over again, to gawk at things that had been familiar once and might be familiar again, after her heart had stopped pounding in her chest, after her head had stopped spinning with the intoxicating scents of night-blooming flowers and the ashes of the day's food vendors.

Vincent's stall was closed up tight for the evening, the shutters sealed, but the scent of fresh-baked pie lingered, lifting her up and steadying her. No food she had eaten in her own world had tasted as good as his pies—no other food in the Goblin Market, either. There might be healthier meals, more balanced meals, more nuanced meals, but his pies were the first things she'd eaten upon finding this wonderful place, upon making her first real friend, and to her, they would always taste like coming home.

She touched the weathered wood of his counter, thinking of the pencils in her pocket, and smiled to herself. Moon must have gone through the last of the pies Lundy had bargained for by now, even if she'd managed to talk Vincent around to giving her Lundy's share after a "short visit" home had turned into more than two years. Lundy's smile faded. More than two years. Who knew if Moon was even still here? So much had changed. *She* had changed. Who was to say anything was the same?

Barely conscious of the decision, Lundy broke into a run. Her clumsiness fell away as she stopped focusing on her feet, until she was loping easy on her newly lengthened limbs, cutting across the Market toward the one place she was almost sure would still be there. The Archivist was a rock, a monument to stability in this place, where things changed every day, but the rules were immutable.

"Be sure," she whispered as she ran. "Be sure, be *sure*. I *am* sure, I swear I am."

The Market didn't reply to her convictions. It surrounded her, engulfed her in the creak of wood and the rustle of canvas, in the slow settling of the dark, which had its own, subtle sound. That was the only reassurance it could give.

Lundy ran down once-familiar trails turned strange by the passage of time, catching her toes on tree roots and stumbling through mud puddles. It was only the knowledge that without her shoes she'd have nothing to barter for a new pair that kept her from stripping the hated things off and throwing them away, to be found by one of the scavengers who worked the edges of the Market. She was no longer the tough-footed child she thought herself to be; if she wanted to be that girl again, she would need to change by stages, to have something thick and safe to fall back on. Not these shoes, perhaps, but another pair, one better suited to her feet, one she had chosen.

She ran, until the Archivist's shack appeared in front of her like a promise fulfilled, lantern-light slipping out through the cracks in its roughly hewn walls. She stopped, gasping for breath, her heart hammering hard against her ribs. This was it, then; this was where she found out whether she had been gone too long to ever be welcomed home.

"Be sure," she whispered, and took a step.

"Be *sure*," she said, and took another.

"Be sure," she hissed, a command meant in equal parts for herself and for the night around her, and she was running again, running until she was almost at the door, until that door swung open and the Archivist was there, the Archivist was laughing in surprise and delight and spreading her arms to catch Lundy as the girl who was no longer a child flung herself into them.

They held each other, both of them laughing

and both of them weeping, and if this were a fairy tale, this is where we would leave them, the prodigal student and the unwitting instructor reunited after what should have been their final farewell. This is where we would leave them, and be glad of it, even as Lundy had long since left a girl named Katherine behind her.

Alas, that this is not a fairy tale.

"I made it, I'm sorry, it shouldn't have taken so long, but I *made* it," said Lundy, her voice muffled by the Archivist's shoulder. "I'm sorry."

"There's no need to apologize," said the Archivist, and pushed her out to arm's length, looking her thoughtfully up and down. "How old are you now?"

"Twelve," said Lundy. "About to be thirteen."

"Curfew is almost here, my pretty love," said the Archivist. "But no matter now: you must be tired. I'm willing to accept two hours of cataloging tomorrow night in licu of an hour tonight and an hour then, if you wanted a place to sleep."

Lundy, who had always understood the purpose of chores—even before she'd been sent away to the Chesholm School, where the things that were asked of her in exchange for the room and board that someone else had already paid for had been far from easy, and even further from reasonable—nodded slowly. "I am tired, and that would be very kind of you," she said. "But I want to see Moon before I sleep. Please, where is she? Do you know?"

The Archivist hesitated, and in that pause, Lundy heard everything she needed to know.

"How long ago?" she asked.

"Almost a year," said the Archivist. "She didn't pine for you, but she was still grieving dear Mockery, and with you gone as well, she lost a certain faith in the world's ability to be fair. She thought if it could steal her closest friend, it could steal anything. She stopped believing in fair value, because how could there be fair value when nothing stayed? And when someone doesn't believe in fair value . . ."

The Archivist's silence spoke worlds. Lundy swallowed heavily.

"Is she in the wood?"

"Yes."

Lundy looked toward the trees, which seemed darker and denser than they had only a few short years before. "Could I find her, if I looked?"

"Yes. But without the credit to buy back her heart, it would do you no good at all. She's a wild thing because she chose to be. If she's too far gone to choose to come back again, that isn't your fault. She wouldn't be the first."

"Do the ones who chose feathers over fairness ever come back?"

"Sometimes. Not often, but sometimes."

Lundy felt her pocket, filled with pencils and

144

erasers and ribbons; filled with bits of chalk and golden rings stolen from the locked lost-and-found box in the headmistress's office. She had thought to pay for a lifetime. Now, it seemed, she might pay for a life instead. "Is there a place I can go to buy credit?"

"Yes," said the Archivist. "But first, sleep, and wake to a new morning. Fill your belly and negotiate its continued fullness. You can't save anyone if you neglect yourself. All you can do is fall slowly with them. Come to bed."

Lundy bit her lip and nodded, and followed the Archivist inside.

The shack had never been large, not even when Lundy herself was much smaller. Despite that, none of its dimensions felt like they had changed. The walls pressed in as much as they ever had; the ceiling was as far above her head as it had ever been. The whole thing seemed to have grown along with her, remaining too small for comfort, remaining large enough to house both her and the Archivist without piling them atop each other.

The fire crackled invitingly. Lundy moved toward it as if in a dream, stretching out on the warm brick of the hearth and closing her eyes. She thought she couldn't possibly fall asleep, not with the Goblin Market all around her, familiar and strange and welcoming her home.

She fell asleep in an instant.

• • •

When Lundy woke, the Archivist was standing by the table, chopping some long, thin-leaved herb that smelled sharp, bitter, and beguiling at the same time. Lundy sat up and yawned, stretching, feeling the knots in her back from sleeping on the stone.

"You'll need a proper bed if you're to stay here," said the Archivist. "You're not a child anymore."

"I suppose not," said Lundy. She touched the patch of feathers on her neck. They remained smooth and real as ever, anchoring her in her skin, in the moment. "I didn't sort my books the last night I slept here. I thought I'd sort them when I got back."

"Then you owe me three hours," said the Archivist mildly.

"Did you know?" That was the question she had carried with her for two years and more in the "real" world.

The Archivist shook her head. "I had no idea. We have a bargain: unless we've discussed modifying it, like we did last night, I trust you to take care of your side of things."

"If you didn't know, how did the Market know? I was tired. I forgot."

"That's why it was a small debt," said the Archivist. "A few feathers? That's practically a reminder. A string around the thumb. It's not until your toes go webbed or your eyes change colors that you have a lot to pay off. If you had decided your freedom to do as you liked mattered more than keeping your word to me, you might have received more than a few feathers. It's the intent and the size of the debt that matters, as much as anything else."

Lundy frowned. "So the Market did it."

"Yes," the Archivist agreed. "The people who live here learned long ago that enforcing debts against one another only leads to inequality. An indulgent parent thinks it isn't right to make their precious children pay their fair share, even though everyone else's children pay. A cruel husband makes his wife bear his debts and runs about free of care while she goes draped in feathers. But if the Market, which knows everything done within its boundaries, wishes to keep the rules, there can be no cheating, no imbalance. Only the knowledge that all must contribute."

"It still feels . . ." Lundy paused, struggling with the concept, and finally said, "It feels wrong."

"That's because you don't know what fairness means. You've been in a place that wasn't fair for so long that the things we'd been trying to teach you have been driven back into the shadows. How many ribbons do you have in your hair?"

"One," said Lundy, startled.

"Imagine, for a moment, that I had a hundred

147

ribbons. Now imagine we both wanted something to eat. Not something fancy or special, not something radiant or rare, just cheese and bread and a slice of mutton. Would it be fair to say the price was a single ribbon?"

Lundy frowned. "I . . . I don't know. Can't the person who has the food decide?"

"It's their food, yes, so they get to set a price—but again, we're not talking about a luxury. We're talking about plain food, the sort of thing that keeps body and soul connected. Our imaginary merchant is getting fair value no matter what, because the Market will make sure of it. Is it fair to ask each of us to give a single ribbon?"

"No," said Lundy.

"No," agreed the Archivist. "It wouldn't be fair, because you'd be paying so much more than I would. Fixed prices may be necessary in a world where there is no authority making sure we take care of each other, but here, with the Market to oversee us, we can relax knowing that fairness will be maintained. If our imaginary merchant asked us each for a ribbon, seeing I could pay so much more while you had so much less, the Market would remind them that fairness is a subjective thing, not a fixed target."

"Oh," said Lundy.

"Things will cost more for you now," said the Archivist gently. "You've grown. You're better able to contribute. We don't ask babies to pay for their keep. We don't ask children to do more than they're capable of. We only ask that people respect the hand that feeds them."

"Everything?"

"Not everything," said the Archivist. "It will still only cost you an hour a night to stay here, because I'm accustomed to your company. The bed, however, you will need to buy or build for yourself. Do you remember what I said last night?"

"That I needed to feed myself before I tried to buy Moon's debt," said Lundy. Her jaw set stubbornly. "That doesn't seem fair."

"Doesn't it? Hunger makes us foolish, causes us to make poor decisions without realizing how poor they are. If you want to help her, you need to help yourself first. No one serves their friends by grinding themselves into dust on the altar of compassion."

Lundy wanted to argue, to say that sacrifice was as important as playing fair, but she couldn't find the words. Finally, she huffed softly and asked, "How do I buy debt?"

"There is a stall. You won't have seen it before, because you've never needed it before. Look for a blue flag with a white star in the lower left-hand corner. The person working there will be able to tell you how much it will take to buy Moon back. Even after you've asked for and received the figure, you're under no obligation to pay, or to pay in full."

"I'll pay," said Lundy stubbornly.

The Archivist sighed. "Yes," she said. "I suppose you will. Run along now, and I'll see you when you return for your three hours' sorting before sleep."

That was a debt that felt increasingly stiff against her skin, making the feathers on the back of Lundy's neck prickle and rise. An hour a night was manageable; three hours would be exhausting. But she owed it, and the Market wouldn't allow her to leave her debts unpaid. Fair value would be enforced.

In a strange way, she found that reassuring. As long as she tried her best and paid attention to the cues the world was giving her, she would always be treating fairly with people, and wouldn't need to worry they were taking advantage of her—that they were taking the only ribbon from her hair for not enough to eat. It was a strange system. It worked. Lundy nodded to the Archivist and left the shack, starting down the path toward the Market.

Seen by day, the woods were the riot of growth and color they had always been, flowers twining around tree trunks and fruit heavy on the vine. That, too, was fair value, she supposed. Even with as much time as she'd spent here, she had never seen the winter come, never seen a season where the forest wasn't so filled with good things to eat that it was almost like a grocery store. A grocery store where the honey was full of bees and sometimes opossums chittered at you for stealing their fruit, but still. As long as everyone only ate what they needed, there was always enough. Paying someone like Vincent for pies or stews or other things was a matter of wanting, not need.

Birds sang in the foliage, and the air was sweet, and Lundy walked with an unconscious spring in her step, the strain of playing normal child in a normal school sloughing away like mist burning off in the sun.

When she came to the Market's edge she hesitated before she turned and made her way toward Vincent's stall, remembering the Archivist's instructions. He was already there, feeding pies into the oven with practiced efficiency. She stopped and leaned against the counter, watching him work.

Some of the girls at school had been obsessed with unicorns, calling them beautiful and perfect and pure. She supposed she understood why. Vincent was a very pretty man, as long as she only looked at his top half, and a very pretty horse-thing when she looked at his bottom half. Most of the girls at school probably wouldn't have been able to cope with the combination. That made her feel a little smug, like she was appreciating something they couldn't.

Vincent turned, and nearly dropped his tray of pies. "Lundy! You're back. We thought . . ."

151

"I came as fast as I could," she said. "I'm staying for a while. I wanted to talk to you about pies."

"I don't need another sharpener," said Vincent. "But I could do with more pencils, if you have them." He made no effort to conceal the greed in his voice.

It made Lundy want to laugh. It was so *nice* to be back where people said what they wanted, where they trusted in fair value to see that they received it. They knew they couldn't cheat each other without the Market becoming involved, and so they merely desired, openly and without shame.

Then Vincent sobered. "I assume you're only buying for yourself this time."

Lundy shook her head. "No. I'm going to buy Moon's debt after this. She's coming home."

"Are you sure? She wasn't careful after you left."

"That means the debt is partially mine. I didn't give her fair value as a friend. What kind of person goes off 'for a minute' and then doesn't come home?" But her bed had been so tempting in the moonlight, white and clean and so much softer than the floor in front of the fire. The bed had welcomed her, and she had been lost.

Vincent nodded slowly. "You're bigger now. I assume you'd like more pies."

More pies would cost more, would leave her

with less for buying Moon's debt. Lundy was about to say that no, the old bargain would be fine, when her traitorous stomach grumbled loudly. She sighed. "What would it cost, do you think, to double what we had before?"

"Four pies each, every day, for a year?" Vincent thought for a moment before saying, reluctantly, "We could do a straight double on both sides— six pencils for the pies—but it takes more than a year for me to go through that many pencils. You'd have to find another way to pay for a second year."

Lundy dipped a hand into her pocket, coming up with six pencils and offering them to him. "That's still fair value. After a year, I'll have something else I can barter with." What it would be, she had no idea. That was a problem for the future. Right now, she needed to eat, and she needed to save her friend.

"Then it's done. Four pies a day for each of you, for the next year." Vincent had the pencils out of her hand and gone behind the counter in an instant. Then, kindly, he asked, "Would you like to eat before you go to buy Moon's debt?"

"One pie, please. I'll come back for the rest."

He nodded, and pushed a single butter chicken pie across the counter.

It tasted like freedom. It tasted like coming home. Lundy offered her farewells around a mouthful of filling and turned away, scanning the market stalls for a blue flag with a white star in the corner. She didn't see one. She began to walk.

Maybe it was the daylight, and maybe it was the pie in her hand, but some of the stall keepers recognized her now. Their cries of greeting mingled with the cries of those who merely wanted to hawk their wares, and the sweet symphony of it all made her feet light and her heart calm. She ate as she walked, and when the last bite of pie slid down her throat she saw it, the blue banner, the white star. She walked faster.

The stall was dark blue canvas, while the banner was the blue of a morning sky, bright and clean and yet untouched by the day. The flap was closed. Lundy hesitated before parting it, ever so slightly, and calling, "Hello?"

"Enter," said a voice, familiar and regretful.

Lundy stepped inside. The Archivist, dressed in a velvet gown the color of her banner, looked up from the great ledger where she'd been writing sums. Her face, as ever, was kind.

"Welcome," she said. "Did you eat?"

"You're *here,*" said Lundy. "Why are you here?"

"Because someone said they wanted to buy a debt, and I am the Market's archivist in task as well as title," the Archivist replied. "Someone has to be willing to check the sums, on the rare occasions when someone disputes fair value. Someone has to put a face to the balance of things. Why are *you* here?"

"Because I'm someone," said Lundy. "Moon. I want to buy Moon's debt."

"She has quite a lot of it. Are you sure?"

Lundy hesitated. What if she couldn't afford the whole thing? What if she found herself covered in feathers, more bird than human, unable to leave the Market without putting herself in a zoo?

And what kind of friend would she be if that mattered?

"Yes," she said. "I'm sure."

"Then show me what you have."

The things that had seemed so grand and clever when pilfered from the school seemed small and unremarkable now. The ribbons, the pencils, the pieces of copper wire, even the golden rings were lessened as she lay them out, one after the other, for the Archivist's appraisal. Blank notebooks and spare socks and rocks she had found in the forest, she put them all down, until her bag was empty, and she put that next to the lot. For a moment, she considered removing her shoes, but decided against it. The Archivist would tell her if it was necessary.

The Archivist looked thoughtfully at the pile, then back to Lundy. "It is enough," she said finally. "But there will be another, less tangible cost."

"Anything," said Lundy.

"That word, that promise, strike it from your tongue," said the Archivist. "With that word,

155

I could ask for the heart in your chest and the blood in your veins and you could not stop me. There is no value fair enough to warrant an open check. Fortunately, I have no interest in taking advantage of children, especially not children who have entrusted themselves to my care. Here is the price. Listen well, and if you will accept it, sign my book:

"All you have offered, I will have, but I will also have your friendship with Moon. I won't take it right away. I won't need to. You're not children any longer, Lundy, and even if you never say a word, never even imply that a debt exists—even if the Market itself says this was fair value intended and given—Moon will read the debt into your silences. She will create it, and in its creation, create the imbalance that accompanies it. She won't see you as her boon companion anymore, but as someone who owns her. Friendship will fall away, drowned in the sea of her resentment. That is what you will pay to save her. Do you accept?"

Lundy stared at her, stricken. "What? No! We've always taken debts for each other. We've always . . . we've always given fair value. You said a single ribbon didn't have to mean the same thing to different people. This is my single ribbon. It doesn't mean anything near as much as she does. Why do you have to take her away from me if I bring her back?"

"I don't. I won't. Not even the Market will. But she'll take herself, and if you accept that fact now, it will be part of the payment, and she'll owe you nothing when she goes."

"Does it *have* to happen?"

The Archivist, who had seen a thousand friendships become unbalanced by assumptions about who owed who, even when no one walked cloaked in feathers, was silent for a moment. Then, finally, she said, "No. It doesn't have to. You can gamble, if you like."

"Gamble with what?"

"A year. If at the end of a year, you're still friends despite everything, you'll be gowned in feathers and will have to buy your own way back to humanity. If I'm right, and she can't love you innocently once she feels there is no balance between you, you'll owe nothing more."

Lundy stood straighter, squared her shoulders, and said, "I'll sign."

"Yes," said the Archivist. "I knew you would."

12 ON WINGS SO WIDE

We must move on, we must move on, for time grows short and there is so much left to do, but first we will stop to see something of terrible importance. So:

Lundy expected to feel Moon's debt settle on her shoulders when she signed the book, expected it to press in on her and weigh her down. She felt nothing. She looked quizzically at the Archivist, who smiled.

"It's done," she said. "Go to the wood."

Lundy turned and fled, running out of the tent and into the Market, weaving between shoppers and sellers with quick, remembered speed. How easy it was to fall back into the good old patterns, to read the movement of the crowd and know how to dance through it like a dream, causing no one any harm, incurring no unexpected debts! She had been away far longer than expected, but in many ways, this was where she had grown up, and would always, always be her home.

At the edge of the Market was the wood. Lundy plunged into it, letting her feet choose the way, until she came to the stream where once she had found a girl with owl-orange eyes weeping by the water. She looked up. She saw neither owl nor girl. She turned in a slow circle, searching still, and so she chanced to see the first feather fall.

This time, when she looked up, it was at a specific tree, and so it was that she saw the feathers falling faster and faster, as what she had taken for a part of the trunk unfolded into a great brown owl, and then unfolded further into a naked, shivering girl.

"Moon!" cried Lundy in delight.

The girl opened her eyes, which were the color of sanded pine, and not owl-orange at all, and stared at her. "Lundy?" she asked finally, in a voice that rasped and croaked and creaked like an unoiled hinge, too long allowed to go unused. "You came back?"

"Can you climb down?" Lundy looked around for something that might soften Moon's fall, if it came to that. All she saw was the stream, which she was fairly sure she couldn't move. "Be careful. I don't want you to hurt yourself."

"How . . . how am I human?" Moon raised one hand, staring first at it, and then at Lundy. "What did you do?"

Fear uncurled in Lundy's stomach, venomous and cold. "I brought you back," she said uneasily. "I'm sorry I was gone so long. You wouldn't have gone to feathers if I hadn't gotten caught

159

and kept in the other world. So I bought your debt and brought you back."

Moon blinked at her. "I owe *you* now?"

"No. No! I bought your debt and I let it go. You don't owe anybody. We get to be human together, we get to be *here* together, so come down from the tree, okay? I've missed you. Please?" Lundy looked at her hopefully, waiting to see what Moon would do.

Moon hesitated. Let us pull back for a moment, and see things through her eyes—for while this is Lundy's story, Lundy's cautionary tale, it might as easily have been Moon's. Pretty, pithy, petty Moon, born to a woman who had left the Market for the comforting climes of a world where fair value was something each person could negotiate for themselves, rather than having it imposed from without by an unimpeachable force of nature. Sweet, sharp, sour Moon, whose true name could never be given because it had been lost, who had seen her world narrow to an owl's understanding of hunt and hole and hover. This story could so easily have belonged to her.

Perhaps it is a pity it did not. It might have had a kinder ending.

She looked at Lundy, who had come to the Market from a world Moon had never seen and never wanted to see, and she asked herself a simple question: could friendship alone be fair value for a debt deep enough to make an owl of a

160

girl? Could friendship balance the scales between them, or would they poison each other, a drop at a time, Lundy trying not to resent what she had spent, Moon trying not to read every request as a command?

Could they ever truly know, if they didn't at least try?

Carefully, Moon unbent limbs that no longer remembered how to be anything but silent and graceful and now lacked the anatomy for what she wanted them to be. With shaking hands she gripped the tree and began descending. She was almost to the ground when she lost her grip, slipped, and fell, only to find her landing softened by Lundy, who dove to save her friend.

Moon blinked at Lundy. Lundy blinked at Moon. Both of them burst out laughing, huge, relieved laughter, the kind of laughter that seemed like it ought to be big enough to fill the world. They clung to each other, and they laughed, and it seemed, for a time, as if they were going to be all right: nothing was going to change, even as everything around them was changing. Lundy removed her school jacket and draped it around Moon's shoulders, giving her a scrap of privacy, and the two girls walked hand in hand to the Archivist's shack, ready to face the future, so long as they could face it together.

The year that followed was a good one, maybe the best Lundy had spent within the Market, which had always been such a source of joy and wonder for her. Every life should contain one perfect year, if only to throw the rest of it into sweet relief, and this was Lundy's. She sorted books for the Archivist; she filled her belly with berries from the forest and pies from the stall. She covered Mockery's grave with flowers, she quested and she questioned and she grew. She listened, she looked, she learned. She paid attention as if it were the dearest coin in all the land, and everyone who spoke to her, even for a moment, said she offered fair value with her listening, which was as canny and clever as the rest of her.

Some in the Market began murmuring about apprenticeships when they saw her walking through the stalls on some errand or the other, having purchased a bedframe with her stockings and school blazer, having purchased the right to store it in the Archivist's shack with two additional hours a week. It was a small thing, to have a safe place to spend the night, to know that she and Moon were warm and well protected.

Moon, seeing the growing closeness between the Archivist and Lundy, seeing the way Lundy could tease meaning from books that seemed like so much useless scribbling to her, considered the merits of jealousy. The Archivist had been her friend and surrogate parent first, after all: Lundy was stealing moments of praise and affection that should have belonged to *her*. Only it wasn't theft, not really, because the moments Lundy took were the moments Moon had never wanted. No words on a page could hold her interest the way the wide world could, and even if Lundy stayed forever—and more and more, it felt like Lundy was going to stay forever—she would never really understand fair value, not all the way down into the marrow of her bones. One of them needed to find a profession that let her bring home material things, food and clothes and maybe, someday, a place to live that wasn't shared with the Archivist.

Moon spoke to Vincent halfway through the year, asking whether he'd ever considered the virtues of an apprentice, someone to sweep the floors and trim the piecrusts. To her surprise, he took her on. To *his* surprise, she proved to be a quick study and an efficient worker, those clever hands pinching pies closed and learning the intricacies of folding dough. Inside of a month, the pies Lundy had bargained for were supplemented with other rewards, little things to give fair value for Moon's labor, with the understanding that, if she continued as she was, one day she'd be able to feed her entire small, strange family through her efforts alone.

Everyone should have a perfect year. The two girls fell in and out of minor debts, with the Market and with each other; they laughed when they found feathers curving along the lines of their hips or tangled in their hair, they scowled when their lips hardened, and always, they worked and they played and they gave fair value as best they could, until there were more debtless days than otherwise, until it seemed like things would be good forever.

Until the day Lundy rose and started for the door, intending to go to the stream and wash her face before she started making plans for breakfast, and the Archivist called, "Wait."

Lundy turned obediently to face her. It was the two of them alone: Moon had left them at dawn, off to help Vincent prepare for the day. "Yes?"

"Do you know what today is?"

Lundy frowned thoughtfully. "It isn't my birthday," she said. "It isn't Moon's finding-day, either, and if you have a birthday, you've never told me what it is."

"It's been a year and a day since you came back to us," said the Archivist. Then, with deep sorrow, she said, "It's been a year since you bought Moon's debt."

Fear uncurled in Lundy's stomach. Feathers were only funny when they were something to be set aside. "Already?"

"Already, and she still loves you." The Archivist looked at her sadly. "You know what that means."

Lundy wanted to argue, wanted to say it wasn't

164

fair, that she wasn't ready, that she had offered fair value each and every day since her return, and she should have earned herself free. But that wasn't the bargain, and a bargain was like a rule, wasn't it? Rules existed to be obeyed, to protect people from a world where no one knew what to do or how to do it.

"What happens now?" she asked.

"It will be easier if you undress," said the Archivist.

Lundy did, removing each article of clothing and setting it aside, until she stood naked in the middle of the room. She looked at the Archivist.

"Will it hurt?"

"No," said the Archivist, and held out her arm, as a falconer might hold out their glove. Lundy felt a sudden burning need to go to it, to follow this rule as she had followed all the rules before—because there had never been a specific *rule* against going through an impossible door into a world that wasn't, had there? She had always been a good girl, even when it hurt her. Now, being a good girl meant going to that hand.

So she did. Flight came naturally, and when she landed, she grasped the Archivist's wrist with as much delicacy as her talons allowed. The Archivist stroked her beak and sighed.

"You can carry messages; you can catch fish," she said. "You can buy your way back. If someone asks if you'd like them to keep your

165

credit, tell them yes however you can and collect it all at once, to shed feathers and find feet, not be caught in the in-between. Do you understand?"

Lundy screeched agreement. The Archivist walked to the door, opened it, and held out her arm. The sun was warm, oh, the sun was warm on Lundy's feathers. She shrieked, once, and she was gone, wings beating at the air, all the sky below her.

"Try to remember you want to come home," said the Archivist, and closed the door.

PART IV
WE FIRST MUST GO

13 ONE MORE DOOR

Lundy collapsed, unfamiliar legs shaking, unfamiliar hands clutching at the dirt as she tried to remember what it meant to have fingers, to have thumbs, to manipulate the world with something other than beak and talons. The Archivist spread a blanket over her narrow, naked shoulders; Moon put a plate with two small pies down in front of her.

"Welcome home, Lundy," she said, her voice full of tears. "I'm sorry."

"How . . . long?" rasped Lundy. Time had been strange to the eagle she had been, seeming to ebb and flow according to its own whims, and not to any logical progression.

"A year," said Moon. "You were gone for a year."

A year was a very long time. Lundy picked up a pie, noting that her fingers were longer, not because she owed anything, but because her *hands* were longer, because everything about her had stepped closer to adulthood while she was flying above her own life. She took a bite. Her stomach, no longer accustomed to cooked food, attempted to revolt. She swallowed anyway, forcing the food to stay down.

A year. She was fifteen. The idea was ridiculous. How could *she* be fifteen? It didn't make sense, but there it was, and Moon had never lied to her. Lundy took another bite of pie.

She'd been almost thirteen when she'd gone through the door and back into the Goblin Market. Her family had been wondering where she was for two years. More and more, she thought— no, she *knew*—this was where she belonged, but somehow, disappearing on them without saying goodbye didn't feel like fair value.

"Fifteen," she said. She put down the pie. She stood, wrapping the cloak around herself, and looked at the Archivist. "I have to go back. I have to say goodbye before it's time for me to choose."

"Do you know what you're choosing?"

Lundy nodded. "I do."

"Your father came here before you. He chose differently. If you stay, he'll know what happened. Fair value will be given. Your choice repays his." Because the Market had paid into her, hadn't it? Had fed and sheltered and taught her. By leaving—even if she was allowed to do so—she would take that value with her.

But she had never asked them to make her an investment. She had just gone where the doorway took her. "I have to tell them," she said. "I have to . . . maybe they won't understand. Maybe they can't. But I have to try, or else everything I've ever said to them becomes a lie, and I can't live with that." Her father would understand. Her mother, her siblings . . . they never would. They would keep looking at a hole where a girl should have been, and wondering.

If she was choosing this—and she *was* choosing this—she needed to do it without debts, and without regrets. Anything else would be unfair.

Moon burst into tears. Lundy held her tight, relishing the fact that she had arms to hold a friend, and her eyes were already on the horizon.

She left at sunset. The clothes on her back were too small, and her skin felt too bare. She was no longer accustomed to shoes; she walked barefoot away from the Market stalls, walked until she found the door that had borne her from her childhood home into the home of her heart, and touched the wood.

"I'm sure," she whispered, and stepped through.

The passage seemed smaller, the cross-stitched rules on the walls shabby and faded. She read them as she walked, until she reached the door and let herself out, into a world that stank of car exhaust and poisoned water. Lundy coughed, and kept coughing as she struggled to orient herself.

When she turned, the tree was gone. That was no real surprise. She felt no real concern. The Goblin Market would come back for her when it was time, and she would return to her true home for the last time. She took another breath. This time, it barely burned her throat at all.

It had been so long since she had been here that she no longer remembered the way. Her feet were another story. She closed her eyes and let them lead her, following their sure and steady tread down the path to the sidewalk, down the sidewalk to the street, one turn at a time until she was standing in front of an ordinary, half-familiar house. The car in the drive was unfamiliar, but the bike lying in the yard was her brother's, older now, rusted, recognizable. She blinked. Her brother should have been far too old for that bike. How—

Her sister. Of course. It had been so long, and Diana had always been so much younger, that she had almost forgotten her in the chaos of boarding schools and miraculous escapes and flying away. Diana would be nine years old now, barely older than Lundy herself had been the first time she'd seen a door that bid her to be sure. Old enough for bicycles. Old enough to have forgotten her older sister.

The same age Mockery had been when she died.

Lundy stepped onto the porch, feeling more out of place than she ever had before. She took a deep breath. She knocked.

She waited.

Footsteps approached on the other side of the door. Lundy tugged at the hem of her too-tight shirt, wishing she could make it larger. Large enough to cover her, large as a cloak of feathers. It wasn't so long ago that she would have been able to fly away. It wasn't too late. This had been a bad idea. She could turn, she could run, she could—

The door opened. Her father appeared, haloed by the living room light. Lundy froze, struck silent by the enormity of the moment. They stared at each other, parent and child united for the first, and possibly only, time.

"You came home," he whispered.

The words were a blow. She reeled, shook her head, and replied, "I came *back*. Home is not here."

"Are you sure?"

So much came down to surety. She lifted her chin, looking her father squarely in the eyes, and said, "I was sure even before you sent me away."

They only had so long before her mother came to see what was going on, why the door was open, letting the night air in. Her father stood his ground, looking at her and saying, "It was for your own good, and I could send you away again. I'm your father. I have rights."

"Sending me away would not be giving me fair value."

He flinched: her words had struck home. But

he rallied, shooting back, "Running away has not given this family fair value. Your mother cries herself to sleep every night. *Every* night. She's done it for the last two years."

"Then we bear the debt together." Lundy hesitated. "How do I repay my share?"

"You stay."

"No." She shook her head. "That's asking me to bear the whole thing by myself, to say what you did wasn't a part of it at all. Maybe you could have convinced me to be happy here, if you'd bothered to try, but you didn't. I was lost and I was grieving and you sent me away. I reject your bargain, even as you're trying to reject fair value. Do better."

He stopped, his breath catching, and seemed to look at her, really *look* at her, for the first time. Finally, in a voice as rough and dry as burning paper, he said, "One year. You stay for one year. After the year ends, if you choose to go, I won't stop you. But for that year, you live here. You treat this as your home. You aren't passing through, you aren't killing time. You belong. I won't send you away: you won't run. Do we have an agreement?"

There was a trick there, a trap; there had to be. Lundy tried to see his words from all angles, looking for danger. She was tired and everything around her was terrible and strange; she couldn't find it. Finally, grudgingly, she nodded.

"We do," she said.

He stepped back, holding the door wider to let her pass. There were tears shining in his eyes. Out of kindness, she said nothing, but stepped into the house that had been her home, looking around with open curiosity. So much had changed. So much was the same.

"Daddy, Mom says you need to—" The child who ran into the room could have been Lundy herself, recast in miniature. She stopped dead when she saw that her father wasn't alone, her eyes going wide and round. Finally, carefully, she asked, "Katherine?"

Lundy blinked. Even at the Chesholm School, she had been Lundy, Miss Lundy there and Lundy alone in the Market, but not Katherine. Katherine was the girl she'd left behind.

But she had promised; this was how she paid her debt. She nodded stiffly, and said, "Hello, Diana."

Diana's eyes remained huge. "Daddy?"

"Stay here," he said. "I'm going to fetch your mother." He rushed away with a speed that could only have been born from the sudden, burning need to put distance between himself and his impossible daughter, the one who lacked the good grace to stay gone.

Lundy looked at Diana. Diana looked at Lundy. Diana spoke first.

"Are you staying?" she asked. "Because I miss

having a sister, but I don't want to forgive you if you're not going to stay."

"I am," said Lundy. Not quite the truth: not quite a lie. It would do. For now, it would do.

Diana nodded gravely and walked across the room to fling her arms around Lundy's waist. Lundy gasped, too startled to pull away.

"You *left,*" said Diana, voice tear-filled and accusing at the same time. She pressed her face to Lundy's middle. Lundy felt her too-small shirt growing damp. "You went away and you *left* me, they said you got kidnapped but everybody knew you ran away because no one wants to be friends with the principal's daughter, you could have stayed and you could have helped me, you could have been my friend and you *left.*" Her last word broke into a wail, and then she was sobbing, holding Lundy so tightly that it felt like there wasn't any chance of her ever letting go.

She could have been Mockery; she could have been Moon. A tear ran down Lundy's cheek. As if that were the signal, more followed, until she was sobbing too, bending near-double to wrap her arms around her little sister and hold her with equal, if less crushing, closeness.

"I'm sorry," she whispered. "I had to. I wasn't thinking about you. I'm so sorry. I'm staying."

"Forever?" asked Diana, finally letting go enough to pull back and look at her with enormous, hopeful eyes.

Lundy sensed the trap that was preparing to snap shut around her, keeping her here, betraying the people who were waiting for her back in the Market. "No," she said. "Not forever. I've promised our father I'll stay for a year before I leave again." A year was safe. A year would make her sixteen, still young enough to take the citizenship oath, still young enough to go home. Any longer than that . . .

She was gambling on her father's lingering memory of fair value, on the fact that he wouldn't make a bargain and then break it. If he sent her back to the Chesholm School, or to something else like it, she was finished. The trouble with having a parent who'd used the same impossible door as she had was that he knew how to play the rules against her.

She had agreed to a year. If he didn't let her go, she would escape. She had flown over the Market, catching fish for the fishmongers and gathering rare herbs for the chemist, she had gathered wood in her talons and hunted rabbits and small deer and other prey for the butcher. She had made bargains and kept bargains and earned the trust and friendship of the Archivist, a woman who was almost as old as the Market, or seemed that way. She could do this.

Diana sniffled. "Why don't you want to stay with us?" she asked.

"I'll stay for a year," Lundy repeated. "Isn't

that better than nothing?" Was it fair value for a sister's love? She didn't know. She couldn't know. She'd never tried to make this bargain before.

Diana was still crying when their father returned, their mother trailing, tired and confused, in his wake. She gasped when she saw Lundy, her hands flying to cover her mouth. Lundy, who would have sworn she was done crying, that she had no tears left, began to weep again. Her mother ran to her, and wrapped her arms around her shoulders, crushing Diana between them. For her part, Diana began to cry again in earnest, and the three of them stayed that way, never letting go, for what felt like forever.

Then, with all the speed despair and anger could imbue, Lundy's mother pulled away, raised her hand, and slapped her across the face. The pain was immediate and intense. Lundy gasped and reeled backward, clapping a hand against her reddening cheek.

"How *dare* you?" hissed her mother. "How dare you run—run away? *Twice?* Or is it three times? Were you ever kidnapped to begin with?"

Lundy stared at her, wide-eyed, too stunned to speak.

"I gave you everything, Katherine! I gave you life, and a home, and everything that should have made you happy, and you *left* us! Why? Did someone offer you more?" Her mother shook her head, eyes red and wet from weeping, hands clenched into fists at her sides. "How could anyone ever offer you more?"

Lundy, hand still clasping her cheek, said nothing. There was nothing to say. She had been young and innocent and selfish the first time she'd gone to the Market: she'd never intended to run away. It had been an accident. But the second time hadn't been an accident, and the third time hadn't been an accident, and even if it was all right for her to go and keep going—even if she belonged in the Market all the way down to the bottom of her bones—there hadn't been anything forcing her to *stay* gone.

Her mother raised her hand again, and her father, surprisingly, was there to catch it and pull it down.

"She's home," he said. "We can be a family again. You get to be angry. We all get to be angry. But first, can't we be together? For just five minutes, can't we be together?"

Lundy's mother folded in on herself, almost falling to the floor. Lundy and her father were there. Together, they caught her before she could hit her head, and they held her, four people weeping in the aftermath of adventure, with so much road ahead of them. So much terrible, unavoidable road.

14 PROMISES AND PAPERWORK

Paperwork is a magic in and of itself. It makes spouses out of strangers, makes homes out of houses . . . and makes students out of runaways. Lundy's father left the house the morning after her return, remaining gone for several hours before he came back with a folder in his hand and a pinched expression on his face. He dropped the folder on the table in front of Lundy without saying a word, walking out of the room, leaving her to pick it up and flip through its contents on her own.

Inside, she found a full set of records for the Chesholm School, beginning with her enrollment and ending mid-semester, presumably to reflect her arrival on her family's doorstep. Her grades had remained excellent during this fictional school career, she noted; as her father's child, she supposed he could have envisioned nothing less for her. Not perfect, which would have been noticed—this fictional version of Lundy had a tendency to daydream during history class, a fact that was reflected in her low marks, and did not enjoy physical education—but high enough to command respect.

There were several student IDs for the years she had missed, her name neatly typed and covered by a layer of lamination. Lundy looked at them, feeling disconnected from her own life, and wondered whether the lack of pictures on the school IDs might have been one of the factors that motivated her father to choose it in the first place. He had traveled to the Goblin Market, even if he had rejected it; he knew its temptations, and its consequences.

For the first time, Lundy wondered about her grandparents. She knew her mother's parents were long dead, but what about her father's? Was the door a thing which called to each generation of the Lundy family in turn, bidding them to be sure even before they knew what certainty was? Were they Moon's opposite, the descendants of a Market child who had been cast out, rather than being kept inside?

As a question, it was a good one, and pondering it helped somewhat with stepping back from the reality of the papers in her hands and the promise she had made. Everything was a story, if studied in the right fashion. She resumed her paging-through, and stopped dead as she found a new student ID, this one clipped to a class schedule. *Her* class schedule, for the local high school.

The reason for the high marks was immediately clear. She had been enrolled in all the classes that would be expected for a young lady of impeccable schooling, including home economics and calisthenics. Everything would have seemed perfectly in order, if not for the remedial history class right before lunch. Which made a certain sense: she could explain the history of the Market, but the history of this world remained a mystery to her.

Grimly, she closed the folder and stood. A year. She had promised him a year. She had promised *Diana* a year. She would keep her word; she would give fair value to this family, and she would return to the world where she belonged with a clear conscience, able to say that she had paid all debts. She *would*. No matter how difficult it was, she would do it.

She found her father in his study, which had been Daniel's room when she'd last been in this house. Her room had remained untouched through her entire absence, both at the Chesholm School and in the Goblin Market. It was too small for her now, decorated for an eternal child, and it pressed in around her like the too-tight clothing she had worn home.

(Those clothes had been missing when she woke in the morning, and she suspected her mother had burned them. The clothes she had now were her mother's hand-me-downs, worn soft and tattered by her mother's body, and smelled faintly of lilac perfume. Lundy suspected she would never again smell lilacs without feeling her mother's palm against her cheek, and she didn't mind. Some forms of fair value are less tangible than others.)

"When do I begin?" she asked.

"I have copies of last year's exams," he said. "I've enrolled you. Said your reason for leaving boarding school was an illness that left you unable to handle being away from your family any longer. I also said you might require a bit more recuperation. As soon as you can pass these exams well enough not to attract attention or embarrass me, you'll begin classes."

How quickly he went from "we can be a family" to "don't embarrass me." Lundy looked at him levelly. "Remember our agreement," she said. "One year."

"I might remind you that I am your father, and you are still a child," he said.

"If you did, I might remind you that I was able to escape from a supposedly inescapable campus. I might remind you, further, that you may have had the start of my education, but you haven't had the parts that mattered. If you attempt to break our bargain, I'll think nothing of taking my acquiescence back and running for the nearest place a door might hide. If you seem to be setting up circumstances so you can, I'll be gone before your plan can be put into motion. I came back to pay my debts. Don't cancel them all with cleverness."

Her father looked at her wearily. "What didn't we give you?" he asked. "Where did we fail you, that the Goblin Market seemed like the better answer? Please. I've wondered for years. How did we go wrong?"

Lundy paused before she said, "You knew who you were. You were *so sure* you'd gotten fair value for your life that you never asked what that was going to mean for the rest of us. You spent our happiness to secure your own. I never learned to make friends here. I never learned to be anything but rigid and lonely."

"You're still rigid. You went to a place that elevates rules to the status of holy law, and you quote those rules back at me now as if they have all the answers."

"Because they do." It was so simple. How could he not see it, when it was so simple? "If you give everyone fair value, no one wants. If no one wants, no one has to take. The Market makes sure we don't take advantage of each other."

"The Market doesn't make you *understand*. With the hand of what might as well be a literal god to guide you, how can you go wrong? How can you learn to do better? The people who live there, fighting every day not to fly away on wings they never asked for, they're no better than pets."

"Were you ever dressed in feathers?"

Her father raised his chin, looked her in the eye, and said, "I would sooner have died."

Lundy was silent. If her father guessed at what her silence contained, he gave no sign.

"A year is long enough to go to school," he said. "You need to understand this world if you're ever to consider choosing it over your beloved Market."

Still Lundy was silent. Her father sighed.

"Don't make me out to be a monster here, Katherine," he said. "If I'd never been to the Market, if your father were some . . . some ordinary, hidebound man with no reason to believe in magic, do you honestly think I would have accepted the declaration of a year's homecoming from my fifteen-year-old daughter without protest? You'd be locked up in someplace far less pleasant than that fancy boarding school, under constant surveillance, and you'd never have a chance to go back. I am trying to be fair with you. I'm trying as hard as I can, even though it feels like it might kill me. I'm your *father*. Believe it or not, I love you, and all I want to do is keep you from making a mistake that will tear this family apart."

"Why would it be a mistake?"

It was his turn to be silent. Lundy scowled.

"If you know something, *tell* me," she said. "Is this about the curfew? Do you know something about it? Can you tell me?"

"Of course they never told you," he said bitterly. "Why should they? They already had you. It means once you turn eighteen, you've chosen by not choosing. You've been living out a countdown since the day you found your door. Unless you take the citizenship oath before your birthday, you can't take it at all, and if you attempt to stay past the cutoff, you'll be punished."

"The Market has to let me stay if I'm in debt," said Lundy. "We'd have heard about it if people with feathers they could never get rid of kept popping up." Still, a worm of unease worked its way down the back of her neck. Feathers might be the way the Market tracked currency, but they weren't exactly a punishment. She had no idea what a punishment might be.

"The Market doesn't *have* to do anything," corrected her father. "The Market is not the friend you think it is. If it were, why would it prey on children, instead of letting us keep coming into adulthood? It wants the young. It wants the malleable. If it wants you, it's because it sees something in you that it can use. Your life is the biggest bargaining chip you have. Before you choose where to spend it, be sure you understand what you're getting in return."

For a moment, it looked like he was going to continue. Instead, he caught his breath, held up his hand, and said, "If you'll excuse me, I took today off, but I still have to finish some paperwork before we go shopping. You'll need new clothes before you can begin your classes."

"What about the exam?"

186

"I'll test you tonight," he said, and turned back to his desk.

Understanding a dismissal when she saw one, Lundy walked away. She closed the door behind herself.

It would have been easy, standing alone in the front room, to keep going. To walk to the front door, open it, and head down the sidewalk toward the nearest copse of trees. It would have been *easy* to announce her sureness to the air and wait for the door to appear. Lundy bit her lip, looking at the window. Not many people knew she was back. It would be relatively easy to cover up another disappearance. The final disappearance. This time, she was going for good.

The door opened. "Katherine?"

Lundy jumped, unable to stop herself. Diana looked at her solemnly, the doorknob still in her hand.

"You're thinking about leaving again, aren't you?" she asked. "Where do you go? Why do you keep leaving me behind?"

Because if you were meant to find the Market, the Market would have found you, Lundy thought. Aloud, she said, "A place that's not like this. D . . . Dad made me promise not to talk about it." The word was slippery on her tongue. She hadn't used it in so long. On the few occasions when she'd needed to discuss him in the Market, he had been "my father." Nothing more personal.

"He doesn't like it when people ask where you are," admitted Diana. "I don't like it either. It always makes me remember that you're not here with me. Are you hungry? I usually make a peanut butter and marshmallow fluff sandwich when I get home. Mom says they'll rot my teeth, but she's still at work, so I don't care."

"Mom got a job?"

"After you went to boarding school. I was in kindergarten, and she said it would 'take the edge off' being alone in the house all day." Diana shrugged. "She's the secretary at the power plant. She likes it okay, or says she does, and she likes being able to buy the name brand stuff at the grocery store. Did you want a sandwich?"

"Sure," said Lundy hollowly. She trailed Diana to the kitchen, watching as the familiar stranger who was her sister began pulling things out of cupboards. Everything was so different now, and so much of it looked the same, which somehow made the differences even worse. She couldn't trust where her memory put things. Either they had been moved, or she had misremembered, but either way, this might as well have been her first time in this house.

She realized she was calculating the value of the knife Diana used to spread the peanut butter on the bread and turned her face away, ashamed.

These things weren't hers. She had come back to steal once, when she'd been younger and less equipped to understand that a thing being in her house didn't mean she had a right to it. This time, she had come back to say goodbye. Fair value for robbing this family of a daughter was a year, nothing more. Certainly not a year and all the silverware.

"Do they have peanut butter and marshmallow sandwiches where you've been?" asked Diana casually.

Lundy raised her eyebrows. "You're trying to trick me into telling you."

"Well, yeah." Diana slapped creamy goo onto the right sides of two pieces of white bread. "I don't like secrets. Everything's been secrets, all the time, since you disappeared. Where's Katherine, where'd she go, did she run away or was she kidnapped, oh she's back, where's she been, now she's off to boarding school, why, why, *why?*" She stabbed the knife back into the jar with more force than strictly necessary. "I guess it's good, since I was so small when you went, and this way I never got to forget you. But it's stupid. We're a family. I should have been allowed to know stuff. I should be allowed *now*."

Lundy looked at her, seeing the similarities between them, seeing the differences. Diana was sharper than she'd been at that age, a knife poised to slice into the world and keep slicing until it gave her what she needed. Lundy had always been more of a needle, careful and precise, following the lines laid out by the rules, never stepping over them. Perhaps that was why the Market had come for her, and not for her sister. Perhaps it had known it could never give Diana fair value.

"I'm sorry," she said. "I can't. I promised."

"Like you promised to stay for a year?" Diana dropped the knife and folded the pieces of bread viciously in half, pressing the marshmallow hard against the peanut butter. "That's *nothing*. You won't see me get to high school, or be there to talk to me about boys, or *nothing*. You might as well not have come back at all if you're only going to come back for a year."

"It's what I have," said Lundy weakly.

"No, it's not." Diana turned, thrusting one of the folded-over sandwiches at her like an accusation. Lundy took it. "You have your whole life. You have my whole life. Two whole lives that we could spend being sisters, and you're going to give me a year. That's not fair."

"You don't really know me."

"You've never *let* me." Diana glared. "A year isn't anything."

"Tell that to the calendar," said Lundy. The sandwich was heavy in her hand, weighted down with sweetness. "Are we going to spend the whole year fighting? Is that what's going to make it okay for you to let me go?"

"I don't want to." Diana nibbled on the edge of her sandwich. "I'd rather be sisters."

"What does that mean?"

"I don't know." Diana shrugged. "I've never had one before."

Lundy smiled. "So let's find out."

The exams were easier than Lundy had feared. Either her halting patchwork education in the Archivist's shack had been more extensive than she'd realized, or the schools of this world were woefully unchallenging for their students. Whatever the explanation, she passed them all, save for the history exam—and as her father had been expecting that, she was already set to be nestled snugly in the bosom of the remedial history class, where her lack of knowledge about current and past events wasn't as likely to trip her up.

Monday morning, she found herself bundled into the back of her father's car, belted in next to Diana, who was fiddling with her slide rule. She didn't object to the seating arrangement. She had never, in all her life, been allowed to ride up front, which was a privilege reserved for adults and older brothers. It would have seemed too strange to be seated there now. It would have seemed like she was claiming an adulthood she didn't really want.

The school, which was dauntingly, terrifyingly

full of bodies—other students, some of whom remembered her as "Katie from my second-grade class," more of whom remembered her as "that girl who disappeared," and most of whom didn't remember her at all; teachers who'd been told to treat her gently after her recent, if fictional, illness—and hallways and classrooms, all of which seemed to be the wrong one.

But there were also books, and lessons, and rules. Rules she could learn and, after learning, follow. Diana was still at their father's school, enduring the scorn of students who didn't want to be seen with the principal's daughter, but here, at high school, Lundy could finally move among her peers without being singled out. She was another student, strange, unfamiliar, but one of them. Ordinary. Normal.

She had been extraordinary as a child, when she had too much authority hanging around her solitary shoulders, and extraordinary in the Market, where she was a summer person and a quester and the girl who'd helped to slay the Wasp Queen, who'd fought for the safety of their borders even before she was a citizen. Ordinary was a novel experience for her. In what felt like the blink of an eye, she had been attending school for weeks, learning her lessons and the nature of her peers, finding the rules that bound them as well as the rules that bound her education.

At the same time, she was learning her sister.

Let us speak, for a moment, on the matter of sisters. They can be enemies to fight or companions to lean upon: they can, at times, be strangers. They are not required to be friends, or to have involvement in one another's lives, or to be anything more than strangers united by the circumstances of their birth. Still, there is a magic in the word "sister," a magic which speaks of shared roots and hence shared branches, of a certain ease that is always to be pursued, if not always to be found.

Even more adroitly than she studied her lessons and the rules of this familiar, suddenly strange world, Lundy studied her sister.

Diana didn't care much for reading, but she had a deft hand with a pencil, and her pastel drawings were years ahead of anyone else in her class. She liked to ride her bicycle, and had chafed for years under restrictions that hadn't existed when Lundy was a child—restrictions she suspected were her fault. Diana had a sweet tooth, didn't enjoy beets, loved to paint her toenails brighter red than her father approved of, and did the dishes without complaining, but hated to wash the windows. She was a *person*. Lundy supposed she always had been. It was just the difference in their ages that had kept her from seeing it before.

More importantly, Lundy liked her. Diana was blunt and funny and pointed when she needed to be; she reminded Lundy of Mockery, only younger, and still alive, and gloriously *here*. She planned to be an artist, to travel the world and see her work hanging in the finest galleries, in the most prestigious museums.

Her face had fallen after the first time she'd admitted her goals, and the look she'd given Lundy had been half love and half loathing.

"I guess that won't happen, though," she'd said. "Once your year's up, you're gone, and I'm back under lock and key."

"Sixteen isn't eighteen," Lundy had replied. "They'll understand."

And they did, that was the beauty of it: when her year ran out and she went looking for the door she knew was there, she found the Archivist and Moon waiting for her at the portal's end. Moon was smiling when Lundy stepped through. Then she looked at Lundy's clothes—clean and tight and ill-suited for running through the trees—and her empty hands, and her smile dimmed, and died.

"Oh," she said, softly. "So *that's* how it's going to be." She handed Lundy the pie she'd been holding, and turned, and walked away.

Lundy, stunned into silence, watched her go. Only when Moon was out of sight did she look to the Archivist, and say, "Her eyes. They're almost brown."

"She's giving and getting fair value, every day," said the Archivist. She looked carefully at

Lundy. "Sixteen years. Are you here for good?"

Lundy looked down at the pie in her hands. "My sister's birthday is next week," she said. "I promised her I'd come to the party. But I'll come back afterward."

"Oh, child." The Archivist reached out and touched her cheek, gentle as a whisper, so far from her mother's slap. "There will always be a birthday. There will always be a holiday, or a funeral, or a birth. If you delay, you can delay yourself right over the edge of being sure."

"I *am* sure," Lundy protested. "I just need a little more time."

"Good," said the Archivist. "There is only a little time left."

Lundy turned and walked back into the passage. The Archivist, who had seen this all before, watched her go.

15 FAIR VALUE

It can be easy, when hearing about someone else's adventures in a far-off, magical land, to say "I would never choose the mundane world over the fantastical. I would run into rivers of rainbow as fast as my legs would carry me, and I would never once look back." It is so often easy, when one has the luxury of being sure a thing will never happen, to be equally sure of one's answers. Reality, it must sadly be said, has a way of complicating things, even things we might believe could never be that complicated.

Lundy returned to her family. Celebrated her sister's birthday. Her mother, whose eyes had lost some of their hollowness, baked a lemon cake, as she had so very long ago, when Diana had been a dream inside her stomach, and Lundy had been a quiet, reserved reality.

Daniel came home on leave from the Army. He stared at Lundy like she was some sort of miracle, and when he asked her if she'd be there when he came home for Christmas, she answered "yes," before she could think twice.

Her seventeenth birthday came and went in a

flurry of gifts and cards, in an increasing warmth that seemed to sweep through the house as every day took them further from the time when she had been a phantom, and not a figure.

Three times Lundy returned to the Market, slipping away on an unguarded afternoon—for they were less careful of her now than they had been, now that they were starting to accept the reality of her—and three times Lundy left the Market for the comforts of her childhood bed, for the companionship of her sister, who had grown in so many fabulous and unexpected ways, who needed to be protected from the rigidity of their father, from the hovering anxiety of their mother. Three times the Archivist met her at the end of the passage, reminding her each time that she would be eighteen sooner than she thought.

Three times Lundy said, "I know. I'm still trying to give fair value," and walked back through the passage, back to the life she had willingly abandoned at eight, and eleven, and thirteen. She never made a *choice*. She never said "this is the day I settle forever in a world I said I didn't want."

She never needed to.

She was standing in the kitchen, looking at the calendar, counting the days before her eighteenth birthday, when her sister came charging into the room and stopped, looking from Lundy to the calendar.

Finally, in a small voice, Diana asked, "Are you going away again?"

"I have to." Lundy turned to face her. "I don't . . . I don't belong here, Diana. Everything is wrong. The water and the air and the way people stand, the things they say . . . it's like I've been on a very long journey, and it's been splendid, it really has, I've learned so much, and I've loved getting to know you better, but I can't stay. I miss my home."

She had never been much of a storyteller. If she had been, she might have been able to explain a little better how many things went into the idea of "home." Not just the taste of the water and the scent of the air, but the way the berries ripened, going from white to purple-black overnight, so the undergrowth was constantly changing. The sound of wings, and never knowing whether any bird was a citizen who'd gone too deeply into debt or something born to feather and sky. The security of understanding that the Market would correct any imbalances fairly and quickly, never privileging one side over the other.

Even the shapes of the people here were wrong. She was far from the only human in the Goblin Market, but it was so strange to walk down the street and see only bipeds, only people with two arms and two legs and a single head and no wings or tails. It was difficult not to yearn for comforting variety, rather than this sometimes-shocking homogeneity.

Diana's eyes filled with slow and terrible tears. "I thought you loved me."

"I do love you, Diana, I genuinely do, but the place I belong . . ." She hesitated. "If I don't go back before I turn eighteen, I can't go back at all. I can't imagine growing old in this world. I'm sorry, I can't. If I stay any longer, I could be trapped."

"I wanted . . ." Diana shook her head. "I wanted you to see me go to high school. I wanted a sister. Can't you stay and be my sister?"

Lundy hesitated. Then, finally, in a small voice, she said, "I can try."

See her now as she was then, almost a woman, still technically a child, running, running, through the trees, a shopping bag filled with every- thing she could grab—forks and spoons and candlesticks, lace doilies and roller skates— thumping against her hip as her feet pound against the soil. How she runs, Katherine Lundy, sweet seventeen and running out of time.

How she ran.

She reached the door, flung it open, flung herself inside, past the rules and through the passage, out into the evening air. It smelled sweet; it smelled like home.

She kept running.

The shutters were open at Vincent's pie stand. Moon, who had somehow become a young woman while she wasn't looking—while she was away doing the same in a foreign land—lifted her head from the dough she'd been kneading, surprise slowly bleeding into delight.

"Lundy!" she cried. "Are you home? Are you finally home? I was so worried, I thought—"

"I need to stop," said Lundy.

Moon blinked. "What?"

"I need to *stop*," repeated Lundy. "My sister, she's not ready to let me go, and the Archivist said I had to take the oath before I turned eighteen. If I can stop getting older, I won't turn eighteen. I need to stay where I am for a little while, until Diana can let go, and I can come home. Please, will you help me?" She held up her bag. "I'm prepared to give fair value."

"I—"

"Please."

Moon stopped. In a small voice, she said, "Follow me." Then she turned, not bothering to remove her apron, and walked away from the dough on the counter.

Lundy followed. Together, not quite side by side, they walked the length of the Market, until they reached a familiar trail, until a small, rickety shack came into view. Moon stopped. Lundy looked at her curiously.

"This is as far as I go," said Moon. "You were my best friend ever. Remember that, okay? I loved you a lot. Even if you did build a boat big

200

enough to bury yourself in." Then she turned and walked away.

Lundy blinked after her for a moment before she started, cautiously, toward the shack. The door was closed. Opening it seemed wrong; instead, she raised her hand, and knocked.

The door swung open. The Archivist was there. Wearily, she looked at Lundy, and asked, "It's to be this, is it? What have you come to ask me for?"

"I . . ." Lundy took a breath. "My sister needs me. I don't want to turn eighteen. I need to wait. Can you help me wait?"

"Lundy—"

"Please."

"What you're asking for isn't what you want. Come *home*. Stay with us. Be safe and happy and stay."

Lundy, lover of rules, lover of *loopholes,* shook her head. Like a dog with a bone, she had found her solution. "No. If I don't turn eighteen, the curfew doesn't apply. I can stay. Please."

The Archivist closed her eyes for a long moment. When she opened them again, the weariness was gone, replaced with sorrow. "Can you give fair value?"

Silently, Lundy held out her sack of stolen trinkets. The Archivist took it, ran her hand through its contents, and sighed.

"Wait here," she said, and vanished into the

shack. When she returned, she no longer held the sack. Instead, she held a small vial the color of a ripe strawberry, carved from a single bright crystal. She offered it to Lundy.

Lundy took it.

"If you drink this," she said, "you will not turn eighteen. But it isn't . . . Please. You asked a question, and you paid the price of it, but please. There will be consequences if you do this. Stay. Please. Just stay."

"Whatever the consequences are, I'll pay them," said Lundy, and opened the vial, and drank.

It tasted like water. It tasted like nothing. It tasted like tears. Again, the Archivist sighed. Lundy looked at her. She was crying.

"The rules are the rules," said the Archivist. "They were set for a reason. I set them for a reason."

Lundy's eyes widened. "What?"

"Names have power, child," said the Archivist. "Titles, too. They call me 'the Archivist' because it would be an insult to call me by my name. But I was here first, and I will be here last, and the Market lives because I am its heart. I loved you so much. I truly did."

"I don't . . ."

"I asked you to remember the curfew, and you did, you *did,* but you didn't give me fair value for it, because you forgot Mockery." The

202

Archivist—the Market—seemed to shimmer, and for a moment she was a girl with white feathers tangled in her hair, a sign of the swan she could have been, if she had lived, if she had been given time enough to grow. "You forgot that sometimes, fair value comes from change, and death, and sacrifice. You can't have everything and give fair value. You can't stop your clock and expect to stay a part of the world. You've followed the rules, my love, my little Lundy, but you've betrayed them at the same time, and your punishment is the punishment that has awaited all rulebreakers, for a broken rule pains us all. Banishment. Go."

Lundy's eyes went wide. "How will I get the potion to start me aging again?"

The Market smiled, heartbroken. "You don't."

She closed the door.

Lundy tried to reach for it, and found she couldn't move; couldn't breathe. Couldn't do anything but stand there, struggling against the air, until she turned on her heel and fled, running back the way she had come.

None of the people she passed would look her in the eye. Vincent's stall was shuttered; Moon was nowhere to be seen. Lundy ran on, fighting against the ache in her lungs, the rejection she could feel from every side, until the door was there, slamming open to admit her.

There was no release even in the passage,

which pressed down against her like it was trying to force her out. She stumbled to the final door, tumbled out into the dust, and fell to her hands and knees, gasping.

When she had her breath back, she looked behind herself. The door was gone.

"I was *sure*," she whispered, and all was silence.

Epilogue
COME BUY, COME BUY

1990

The woman, who appeared to be in her early fifties, and was dressed like she had never met a color she didn't feel compelled to keep somewhere on her person, stepped out of her car and considered the house. It looked perfectly ordinary in every possible way, as did the town around it. She knew better. She paid attention, which was sometimes the dearest coin of all, and she had heard the rumors, the stories of a little girl who aged, not forward as children are intended to do, but in reverse, slow as the hands of a clock running backward.

(One of those rumors had come in the form of a letter from the girl's younger sister turned older and wiser and sadder. "My sister disappeared when she was a child," the woman had written. "Now my son has done the same, and I think it's happening again, and she still needs someone to save her . . .")

"Well," she said, and started up the walk. The doorbell was in good repair; the sound it made rang out clearly. Settling on her heels, she waited.

The door opened, just a crack, several minutes later. "My parents aren't home," said the girl on the other side, who couldn't have been more than fourteen years old, but who had the eyes of a woman grown and condemned.

"I know, dear," said the woman. She smiled, clearly trying to be engaging. "My name is Eleanor West. I've been looking for you for quite some time, Miss Lundy. I think we're going to be very good friends, you and I."

Slowly, Lundy pulled the door open and looked at Eleanor. Neither said a word.

It was not, perhaps, a happy ending. But it was what they had, and so we shall leave them to it as we head on, ever on, toward the next, patiently waiting door.

ABOUT THE AUTHOR

Seanan lives with her cats, a vast collection of creepy dolls, and horror movies, and sufficient books to qualify her as a fire hazard.

She was the winner of the 2010 John W. Campbell Award for Best New Writer, and in 2013 she became the first person ever to appear five times on the same Hugo ballot.

Books are produced in the United States using U.S.-based materials

Books are printed using a revolutionary new process called THINKtech™ that lowers energy usage by 70% and increases overall quality

Books are durable and flexible because of Smyth-sewing

Paper is sourced using environmentally responsible foresting methods and the paper is acid-free

Mount Laurel Library
100 Walt Whitman Avenue
Mount Laurel, NJ 08054-9539
856-234-7319
www.mountlaurellibrary.org

Center Point Large Print
600 Brooks Road / PO Box 1
Thorndike, ME 04986-0001 USA

(207) 568-3717

US & Canada:
1 800 929-9108
www.centerpointlargeprint.com